A deadly secret . . .

"That's ridiculous!" Elizabeth laughed. She had just finished watering the plants and was pouring the remaining water into the kitchen sink.

Jessica grabbed the watering can from Elizabeth's hand and plopped it on the counter. "Is it?" she challenged, her eyes flashing. "Here are the facts." She started counting off on her fingers. "Mr. Clark's side of the closet is empty. Mrs. Clark's side is full. The room looks like Mr. Clark left in a hurry. Nobody seemed to know the other one was leaving. Nobody has a number where they can be reached. The paperboy heard them having an argument. There's a bloody knife in a closet. There's a clump of hair on the hinge of the basement door. There's blood on the floor in front of the door. And we're not supposed to go into the basement! I'm telling you, Elizabeth, something's not right here. And don't tell me there's a logical explanation for it all." Jessica paced back and forth like a caged animal.

"But—," Elizabeth started to protest.

"It's obvious Mr. Clark has murdered his wife and now he's on the run!" Jessica declared fiercely.

1

Visit the Official Sweet Valley Web Site on the Internet at:

http://www.sweetvalley.com

SWEET VALLEY TWINS

Don't Go in the Basement

Written by
Jamie Suzanne

Created by
FRANCINE PASCAL

BANTAM BOOKS
NEW YORK·TORONTO·LONDON·SYDNEY·AUCKLAND

To Traci Ann Heller

RL 4, 008-012

DON'T GO IN THE BASEMENT
A Bantam Book / September 1997

*Sweet Valley High® and Sweet Valley Twins® are
registered trademarks of Francine Pascal.*

Conceived by Francine Pascal.

*Produced by Daniel Weiss Associates, Inc.
33 West 17th Street
New York, NY 10011.*

Cover art by Bruce Emmett.

ISBN: 0-553-48440-0

Published simultaneously in the United States and Canada

Bantam Books are published by Bantam Books, a division of Bantam
Doubleday Dell Publishing Group, Inc. Its trademark, consisting of the
words "Bantam Books" and the portrayal of a rooster, is Registered in the
U.S. Patent and Trademark Office and in other countries. Marca
Registrada. Bantam Books, 1540 Broadway, New York, New York 10036.

PRINTED IN THE UNITED STATES OF AMERICA

OPM   0 9 8 7 6 5 4 3 2 1

One

◇

"Hey, Jessica, look at this!" Elizabeth Wakefield plopped down on the couch beside her twin sister and pointed to an advertisement in her magazine. "There's a computer game that's based on Amanda Howard's books!"

Amanda Howard was Elizabeth's all-time favorite mystery writer. "'Join Christine Davenport as she tries to unravel the mystery of the lost letter,'" Elizabeth read out loud. She flopped back against the couch and smiled, imagining how much fun she'd have playing that game.

Jessica glanced briefly at the magazine in Elizabeth's lap, then turned back to the fashion catalog in her lap. "Whatever," she said in a bored voice.

"Too bad it costs fifty dollars." Elizabeth bit her lip.

"Fifty dollars!" Jessica snorted. "Just for a lousy computer game?"

Elizabeth looked at Jessica's catalog. "I bet the blouses on that page cost that much too."

"They cost a lot more than that," Jessica declared. "These are original Di Giorgio blouses. They come from Italy. If you could find one for seventy-five dollars, you'd be getting a real bargain."

"You call a seventy-five-dollar blouse a bargain?" Elizabeth laughed.

But she knew she shouldn't have been so surprised. Though she and Jessica were identical on the outside, with their long sun-streaked blond hair, blue-green eyes, and a dimple in their left cheek, on the inside they were totally different.

Jessica was into fashion, boys, makeup, and movie stars. She belonged to the Unicorn Club, which was an exclusive club of girls who considered themselves the prettiest, most popular girls at school. Their sole purpose, it seemed to Elizabeth, was to have parties, go shopping, and talk about boys.

Elizabeth didn't mind doing those things *some* of the time, but she didn't want to do them all the time. She needed time for reading, working on the *Sweet Valley Sixers*, which was the sixth-grade newspaper she had helped start, or having long, serious discussions with her friends.

She knew Jessica thought her friends were boring

and immature since they weren't into the same things the Unicorn Club was into. But sometimes Elizabeth thought Jessica's friends were snobbish and silly. So, in a sense, that made them even. The important thing was that the twins had enough in common to be the best of friends, despite their differences.

"I'd give anything to have this blouse in purple," Jessica said, gazing at her catalog. "Lila and Janet would be so jealous!"

"Do you have some money saved up?" Elizabeth asked.

"Money?" Jessica raised one eyebrow. "What's that?"

Elizabeth nodded. "I know how you feel," she said sympathetically. She did some quick figuring in her head. It would take her two months to save up enough money for the computer game she wanted. And that was assuming she didn't go to any movies, buy any ice cream sundaes, or spend any of her allowance at all.

"Face it, Elizabeth, our allowances just don't go as far as they should," Jessica grumbled. She tossed her catalog onto the coffee table and pulled her legs up under her. "I know Mom and Dad said no raise until our thirteenth birthday, but maybe if we talk to them together . . . maybe if we show them just how expensive the basic necessities of life are . . ."

"It wouldn't work." Elizabeth shook her head.

She laid her magazine on top of Jessica's catalog. "Steven tried to get a raise last week and Mom and Dad said no. They said if he wanted more money, he should get a job."

"Well, Steven's fourteen," Jessica pointed out. "There must be, like, thousands of jobs he could get. But we're only twelve. What kind of jobs could we get?"

Elizabeth shrugged. "Baby-sitting?"

Jessica made a face. "Are you kidding? Don't you remember what it was like baby-sitting for the Riccoli kids?"

A few weeks earlier, Elizabeth and Jessica had baby-sat for the four Riccoli kids. All sorts of weird things had happened in that house. That's because a woman who everyone thought had died as a little girl was living in one of the upstairs rooms and tormenting the kids. Elizabeth shuddered at the memory. Maybe baby-sitting wasn't such a great idea after all.

"OK, how about dog-sitting?" Elizabeth suggested.

"That's even more work than baby-sitting. You have to go outside and clean up after the dog." She wrinkled her nose. "No way."

"House-sitting?" Elizabeth tried again.

"House-sitting?" Jessica scrunched up her face.

"Sure." Elizabeth brought her knees up and hugged them to her chest. "You know, when people go out of town we could bring in their mail and water their plants. That kind of stuff."

"That sounds pretty easy," Jessica said with mild interest.

"It wouldn't take very long," Elizabeth mused. "We could probably keep up with several houses at once."

"We could start our own business!" Jessica exclaimed, her eyes shining.

"We could," Elizabeth agreed, growing more excited by the minute.

"This could be really big," Jessica said, rising to her feet. "I mean, everyone goes out of town sometime. I bet we'd get lots of work." She paced back and forth, rubbing her chin.

"Probably more than we'd want," Elizabeth agreed.

"We might even have to quit school to keep up with it all," Jessica said in a serious voice.

"I wouldn't go that far," Elizabeth said, grinning. "But I bet I could get my computer game and you could get your blouse."

"And if we have to quit school, we have to quit school," Jessica said, shrugging.

"So what should we call ourselves?" Elizabeth asked. She and Jessica were sitting at the computer a few minutes later designing a flyer to advertise their new business.

"How about . . . Wakefield and Wakefield,

Professional House-Sitters?" Jessica mused.

Elizabeth tried the name out. "Wakefield and Wakefield. I like it!" She grinned.

"I knew you would!" Jessica grinned back.

Elizabeth chose a large, eye-catching font and typed the name of their business at the top of the screen. "Below that we should list the jobs we're willing to do," she said, turning to her sister.

Jessica counted them off on her fingers. "Let's see . . . we'll bring in the mail and water plants. . . ."

"All right, which one of you stole the *TV Guide*?" Their older brother, Steven, strode purposefully into the room. He lifted the cushions on the couch and searched under the chairs. Elizabeth noticed that the *TV Guide* was sticking out of his jacket pocket, but she didn't say anything.

"What else?" Elizabeth looked up at Jessica. "We need to list more than two things."

"We'll bring in the newspaper," Jessica volunteered.

Elizabeth added that to their list. "And we'll provide peace of mind!" she said brightly.

"That's a good one." Jessica nodded enthusiastically. "Type it in."

Steven walked over to the computer desk. "What are you guys doing?" he asked.

"None of your business," Jessica informed him.

"Yeah, go away, Steven. We're busy." Elizabeth waved him away.

Steven put one hand on Elizabeth's shoulder and the other hand on Jessica's as he leaned down and read what was on the computer screen. "'Wakefield and Wakefield, Professional House-Sitters'? But Mom and Dad already have jobs. Why do they want to become house-sitters?"

"Very funny!" Elizabeth rolled her eyes.

"For your information, Mom and Dad aren't the house-sitters," Jessica told him. She slid closer to Elizabeth. "Lizzie and I are," she said, draping an arm over Elizabeth's shoulder.

"You?" Steven's eyes darted from one twin to the other. Then he tipped his head back and laughed.

Jessica frowned. "What's so funny?"

"Yeah," Elizabeth chimed in, folding her arms across her chest. "At least we're willing to work for our money—unlike *some* people I know."

Steven snorted. "You may be willing to work, but who's going to hire you?"

"Lots of people!" Jessica said indignantly.

"Yeah, right." Steven laughed. "I can see it now. 'Wakefield and Wakefield, Professional House-Sitters. For a small fee, we will lose your newspaper, kill your plants, and destroy your mail.'"

Jessica jumped up, yanked the *TV Guide* out of Steven's pocket, and hit him with it. "Get out!" she yelled. "Out! Out! Out!" She chased him all the way out of the den with the *TV Guide*, then threw it out the door after him. "And don't come back!" she shouted, slamming the door behind him. "Now," Jessica said, taking a deep breath and returning to her chair, "where were we?"

"I think we were getting ready to print out our flyers," Elizabeth said with a twinkle in her eye.

"Oh, good!" Jessica squealed, clapping her hands together. "How many should we print? A thousand?"

Elizabeth laughed. "I was thinking more like ten."

"Ten!" Jessica looked insulted.

"Where are we going to put a thousand flyers, Jess?" Elizabeth wanted to know.

"We'll put them on bulletin boards, street-lights, and cars that are in the mall parking lot," Jessica answered. "And that's just for starters."

Elizabeth thought about it. "I suppose the more we get out there, the better," she agreed. "How about we print out a hundred?"

"OK," Jessica agreed. "We might not be able to handle all the business we'd get from a thousand flyers anyway."

"So when are people going to start calling us?" Jessica asked glumly, her chin resting in her hand.

It had been three days since she and Elizabeth had put out their flyers. They hadn't had a single call yet.

Elizabeth sat down at the table beside Jessica and sighed. "I don't know," she said, sounding just as depressed as Jessica felt. "I would've thought we'd have had at least one or two calls by now." She reached for a banana from the fruit basket in the middle of the table.

"I would've thought more like fifty or sixty calls," Jessica remarked. "Maybe we accidentally put the wrong phone number on the flyer?"

Elizabeth shook her head. "I double-checked everything before we printed them out," she said, peeling her banana.

"Well, maybe there's something wrong with the phone." Jessica leaped up and grabbed the receiver off the wall. There was a dial tone.

Jessica pressed the zero button.

"What are you doing, Jess?" Elizabeth asked, biting into her banana.

Jessica put her finger to her lips. "Hello? Is this the operator? I'm not sure my telephone is working," she said into the phone. "Could you call me right back?" Jessica hung up and waited. After a few seconds she banged her fist on the counter. "I knew it! There's something wrong with the phone!"

"Maybe—," Elizabeth started to say, but a shrill *rrrring* cut her off.

Jessica groaned. She picked up the receiver. "I guess the phone is working just fine," she told the operator dejectedly.

It didn't make any sense. They had handed out a hundred flyers. They had the proper phone number on the flyers. And their telephone was supposedly working. So why hadn't they received a single call?

Elizabeth's heart pounded. It was Tuesday morning and she was sitting outside the principal's office. She didn't really think she was in trouble for anything, but Mr. Clark had called her down right in the middle of English class. *What in the world could he possibly want?* she wondered.

"OK, Elizabeth." Mr. Clark's secretary, Mrs. Knight, smiled at her. "You can go in now."

"Thanks." Elizabeth rubbed her sweaty palms on her jeans and stood up. She walked over to Mr. Clark's office on shaky legs and knocked.

"Come in," said a voice from behind the door. Elizabeth opened the door.

Mr. Clark stood in front of his filing cabinet, rifling through some folders. "I understand you and your sister are running a house-sitting service," he said without even looking at Elizabeth.

"Uh, yeah," she admitted, closing the door behind her. She bit her lip. *Is that what this is about?*

"W-W-Were we supposed to ask permission before hanging up our signs at school?" she asked nervously. She and Jessica had hung one of their flyers in the teachers' lounge, thinking one of their teachers might hire them.

"No, no, no, nothing like that," Mr. Clark assured her. He slammed his file drawer closed and returned to his desk. He pulled open his middle drawer and looked inside. "It's just that I've suddenly been called out of town. I'm leaving in a few minutes. But before I go, I need to find someone to look after my house."

"Oh!" Elizabeth cried, standing up a little straighter.

Mr. Clark finally looked at her. "Now, just a minute," he said, fixing her with a serious stare. "I'm sure you'd do a fine job, Elizabeth. But, well . . . to tell you the truth, I'm a little nervous about your sister. She's . . ." He seemed to be searching for just the right word. "She's not the most responsible student here at Sweet Valley Middle School."

"Oh, Jessica's responsible," Elizabeth assured him. "Really, she is. There was this time she . . ." Elizabeth racked her brain, trying to think of *something* Jessica had done recently to show she was responsible. Something. Anything!

"Yes?" Mr. Clark prompted her.

"Uh, she fixed our neighbor's flowers last

week!" *That sounded good, didn't it?* Elizabeth figured it did as long as she didn't mention the part about Jessica's having to fix the flowers because she had sort of biked through them, smashing them, when she rounded the corner too fast.

They *had* to get this job! If they could get one job, then maybe they could get more.

"Yes, well, responsibility aside, my main concern is, will she follow my directions?" Mr. Clark asked, slamming his middle drawer closed and opening a drawer to his right. He was obviously more interested in finding whatever it was he was looking for than in hearing examples of Jessica's responsibility.

"Jessica's good at following directions," Elizabeth assured him. "If you tell her to do something, she'll do it." *Or at least, I'll do it,* Elizabeth thought. *Just please give us the job!*

Mr. Clark frowned. Apparently whatever it was he was looking for wasn't in that drawer either. He tried another drawer below it.

"What about parties?" he asked, rummaging through one of the bottom drawers. All Elizabeth could see of him was the bald spot on his head.

"Uh, what about them?" she asked tentatively.

Mr. Clark slammed the drawer closed and looked at Elizabeth. "Can I trust you girls not to have a party in my house while I'm away?"

Elizabeth looked shocked. "Of course not! I mean, of course we won't. You can trust us, Mr. Clark!"

Mr. Clark scratched the bald spot on his head and sighed. "Well, it's not like I have much choice." He checked the digital clock on his desk, then slapped his hand to his head. "I should've left five minutes ago."

He stood up abruptly and grabbed his jacket from the coat tree near the door. "Let's see . . . the key! You need a key." Mr. Clark felt his shirt and pants pockets. "Where did I leave my keys?"

Elizabeth had never seen Mr. Clark look so flustered before. He was usually so . . . *together.*

Mr. Clark found his keys in one of his jacket pockets. He took a blue key off the ring and handed it to Elizabeth. "Just follow University Avenue until you get to Mercury Drive. There's a small church on the corner. My house is right next door. This key unlocks the front door." He glanced at the other keys on the ring. "I guess that's the only key you need," he said, putting the other keys into his pants pocket.

"I'll want you to feed the fish, water the plants, bring in the mail, and pick up the paper every day. Can you start this afternoon?" He looked questioningly at Elizabeth as he slipped his arm into his jacket.

"Sure." She nodded. "We can do that." She followed him out to the main office. "How long are you going to be gone, Mr. Clark?"

A telephone rang, and Mrs. Knight picked it up. "Sweet Valley Middle School . . ."

"I don't know," Mr. Clark said absently. "Just keep coming until I'm back at school. Now, is there anything else? Fish, newspaper, mail, plants," he muttered to himself. "Oh! The basement!" he cried, raising his finger in the air. "Don't go down there! It's . . . not safe."

"Sure," Elizabeth said. She couldn't imagine why she and Jessica would go down in Mr. Clark's basement anyway. "Don't worry about anything, Mr. Clark. Jessica and I will take care of everything."

But Mr. Clark was already out the door.

Two

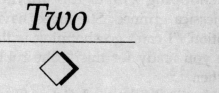

"Ask me why I can't go shopping with you guys after school," Jessica said smugly. It was lunchtime and Jessica was sitting with her friends at the Unicorner, which was the Unicorn Club's special table in the cafeteria.

"I didn't know we were going shopping after school," Ellen Riteman said blankly.

"We're not!" Jessica rolled her eyes. *Honestly! Ellen can be such a ditz sometimes.*

Jessica turned to Janet Howell, who was an eighth-grader and president of the Unicorn Club. "Just pretend we had plans to go shopping after school today and ask me why I can't," she insisted. She couldn't wait to tell everyone!

Janet chewed her hamburger-and-macaroni

casserole about a thousand times before she finally swallowed. Then she dabbed the corners of her mouth with her napkin. "OK, Jessica," she said when she was done. "Tell us why you can't go shopping with us this afternoon."

Jessica grinned. She loved having everyone's attention. "I can't go shopping with you because . . . are you ready for this?" She rubbed her hands together.

Mandy Miller and Betsy Gordon watched her expectantly.

"Tell us already!" Kimberly Haver demanded, tucking her long brown hair behind her ear.

"I have a job!" Jessica announced.

"A *job?*" Lila Fowler said, as though she'd never heard the word before. Jessica figured it was possible she hadn't.

Lila was Jessica's best friend after Elizabeth. Her dad was totally rich. They lived in a huge mansion across town. Anything Lila wanted, Lila got. She had never worked for anything in her life and she probably never would.

"Elizabeth and I started a house-sitting service," Jessica went on. "And we just got our first client." *Never mind that it took almost a week to find a client. That's beside the point.* "And you guys are never going to guess who it is."

"Somebody we know?" Mandy asked, biting into her brownie.

Jessica nodded. "Somebody we know *very* well," she said mysteriously.

"Johnny Buck?" Ellen guessed. Johnny Buck was the Unicorns' favorite singer.

"She wishes!" Lila laughed.

Janet snorted. "Like Johnny Buck would hire *Jessica* to house-sit for him!"

"Who *would* hire Jessica to house-sit?" Kimberly asked snidely.

"Yeah, who is it?" Mandy wanted to know. "Come on, Jessica. Tell us."

The way they were teasing her, Jessica was tempted *not* to tell. But this was too good to keep to herself. She *had* to tell. "We're house-sitting for Mr. Clark!"

"Mr. Clark?" they all squealed at once.

"As in our *principal*, Mr. Clark?" Ellen asked with disbelief.

"That's the one," Jessica said, trying to sound nonchalant. But inside she was enjoying her friends' reaction. "I'm sure he interviewed tons of people for the job, but in the end he decided to hire Elizabeth and me."

"Why?" Lila asked, wrinkling her nose. "I mean, why would he hire you guys?"

Jessica frowned. "Because we were obviously the most qualified for the job." She flipped her hair over her shoulder importantly.

"So you're going to get to see the inside of

his house," Janet said thoughtfully.

"Like, you could look inside his closet and open his drawers and stuff," Kimberly pointed out.

"You can tell a lot about a person by the things they have in their drawers," Mandy said, smiling wryly.

"Or the things they *don't* have in their drawers," Lila added, taking a swallow of milk.

"Well, I'll tell you guys all about Mr. Clark's house tomorrow," Jessica promised. That would be two days in a row she'd be the center of attention. *This job thing is working out OK,* she decided.

"This is so bizarre," Jessica said as she and Elizabeth walked down University Avenue looking for Mercury Drive. "We're house-sitting for *Mr. Clark!* We're going to go inside his house, and we're going to see all his things."

"It's kind of weird, isn't it?" Elizabeth asked. "I mean, I never thought we'd house-sit for people we actually know."

Jessica kicked a pebble that was in her path. "You know how Mr. Clark always wears that same old brown tie? I've been dying to look inside his closet and see if he actually has another tie. And here's my chance!" She giggled.

"Jessica!" Elizabeth cried. "We are *not* going to go through Mr. Clark's things."

"Why not?" Jessica asked, her eyes twinkling

with mischief. "It's not like he's going to be there. He'll never know we did it," she said with a dismissive wave of her hand.

"We're being paid to water his plants and bring in his mail," Elizabeth said sensibly. "And that's what we're going to do."

Yeah, but it doesn't have to be all *we do*, Jessica thought. But she decided not to say it.

"There's Mercury Drive," Elizabeth said as they turned the corner.

"And there's the church." Jessica pointed at a small brick building that sat on a hill.

"So that house over there must be Mr. Clark's," Elizabeth reasoned.

It was a blue house with white shutters and an attached garage. A hedge separated Mr. Clark's yard from the tiny church parking lot.

The twins scampered up the wide steps that led to the house. Jessica picked up the newspaper that was lying on the front stoop, and Elizabeth pulled the shiny blue key out of her pocket and unlocked the door.

"Wow," Jessica breathed, stepping into the house. "This is much nicer than I would've expected. Considering it's Mr. Clark's and all."

The Clarks had obviously hired a professional decorator. The living room was done in mauve and gray. Everything blended perfectly, right down to the knick-knacks on the tables and the pictures on the wall.

"It's weird being in here," Elizabeth said in a low voice. But even though she spoke quietly, her words echoed in the empty house.

"You mean because it's Mr. Clark's house?" Jessica walked slowly through the room, taking everything in. She wanted to make sure she could describe the house in full detail to her friends the next day.

"That," Elizabeth agreed. "And the fact that it's so . . . quiet!"

It *was* quiet, Jessica had to admit. *Eerily* quiet.

"Look! Here's a picture of Mrs. Clark." Jessica eagerly snatched up the frame from the table. It was actually a photo of Mr. and Mrs. Clark together. Mrs. Clark was sitting and Mr. Clark was standing behind her, his hand resting on her shoulder.

"Mrs. Clark is kind of pretty," Jessica observed. The principal's wife had light brown hair that hung in soft curls to her shoulders and a nice smile. "Why do you suppose a woman who looks like that would marry a man like Mr. Clark?" Jessica stuck her tongue out and shuddered.

Elizabeth frowned. "Put the picture back, Jess. We don't want to break anything."

"I'm not going to break anything!" Jessica snapped, replacing the frame. She bumped into the table as she followed her sister into the next room.

"We need to find the fish that we're supposed to feed," Elizabeth murmured, looking around.

It was so quiet that Jessica could hear the ticking of a clock somewhere.

"Well, they're obviously not in here," Jessica said with a wave of her hand. They were in a formal dining area now. The table in the middle of the room was polished to a shine. So was the china hutch that stood against the far wall.

The twins walked silently into the kitchen. This room was done in blue: blue striped wallpaper, light blue countertops. Beside the sink was a wooden block with several long, sharp knives sticking out of it. And beyond that countertop was a door that Jessica figured led to the basement.

Bong!

"Aaaaaah!" Both girls jumped.

Bong! Bong!

"W-W-What is that?" Jessica cried, grabbing her sister's arm.

"I think . . . it's a grandfather clock," Elizabeth said with hesitation. She reached for Jessica's hand and they walked slowly through the other kitchen door out to the living room.

Jessica breathed a sigh of relief. "It *is* a grandfather clock," she said. Somehow they had missed it when they first came in.

"Let's find the fish and get out of here," Elizabeth said.

"OK," Jessica agreed. But just as she was about to turn around, she saw a face pressed against the living room window. "Aaaaaah!" she screamed again.

Elizabeth whirled around. "What?" she asked in a panicked voice.

"A f-f-face!" Jessica raised a trembling finger toward the window, but by then it was gone. "I saw a face."

There was a tapping on the screen door.

Jessica jumped. It was the same face she'd just seen in the window. But the face didn't look nearly so scary at the door as it did at the window.

Jessica felt her shoulders relax. The woman at the door was about their grandmother's age. She wore a green housedress and had curlers in her hair. *Totally harmless!* Jessica chastised herself.

Elizabeth went to the door. "Can we help you?" she asked politely.

The woman tried to see past Elizabeth into the house. "I'm Mrs. Collins, from next door." The woman glanced from Elizabeth to Jessica. "Is Mrs. Clark here?"

"Mrs. Clark?" Jessica went to the door and stood beside her sister. "Didn't she go out of town with Mr. Clark?"

Mrs. Collins's eyebrows flew up in surprise. "Mr. Clark is out of town? Now? In the middle of the school year?" She let out a nervous laugh. "I didn't think Mr. Clark *ever* went anywhere during the school year."

"He usually doesn't," Elizabeth confirmed. "I got the impression this trip was kind of sudden."

"Really?" Mrs. Collins rubbed her forehead in confusion. "Hmmm. Well, do you have any idea where they went?"

Jessica shrugged.

"No." Elizabeth shook her head. "My sister, Jessica, and I are students of Mr. Clark's. He hired us to house-sit while he and his wife are away."

"Well, I've been away myself," the older woman said, glancing around. "Listen, the reason I stopped by is that I have this package for Mrs. Clark. It was delivered to my house by mistake." She held up a brown package the size of a cereal box.

Elizabeth opened the door and brought it in. "I'll set it with the rest of the Clarks' mail," she promised.

"Thanks!" Mrs. Collins waved, then left.

Elizabeth glanced absently at the package, then did a double take. "That's weird," she muttered.

"What?" Jessica asked, closing the door.

"Look," Elizabeth said, holding the package out

for Jessica to see. "It's got 'overnight delivery' stamped all over it."

"So?" Jessica shrugged.

"So look at the postmark." Elizabeth pointed to the ink mark in the upper right-hand corner. "It was postmarked three weeks ago. Don't you think if Mrs. Clark was expecting a package to come overnight, she would've called to check on it before now?"

"Well, it obviously wasn't *that* important," Jessica said with a sniff.

"Where are Mr. Clark's fish?" Elizabeth wondered out loud.

"Why didn't you *ask* him when you talked to him today?" Jessica asked impatiently. The twins were in a short hallway behind the kitchen, staring at several closed doors.

Elizabeth tried the first one. It was just a bathroom. "I thought they'd be right out in plain sight," she defended herself.

"Well, obviously they're *not*," Jessica remarked. She tried the door across from the bathroom.

"What's in there?" Elizabeth asked, coming up behind Jessica and knocking her into a shelf.

Crash!

Jessica drew in her breath. She turned to Elizabeth. "I, uh, think we found the fish," she said weakly.

Elizabeth crowded in beside her and gasped. "They're on the floor!" she cried. The fishbowl was scattered in pieces around them.

"Quick! We've got to find something else to put them in," Jessica shrieked.

"I'll get something from the kitchen," Elizabeth said, running out of the room.

Jessica could hear her sister opening and closing cupboards in the kitchen. "Have you found something yet?" she asked, glancing nervously at the four goldfish that were wriggling on the floor.

"No!" Elizabeth yelled back.

"Well, hurry up!" Jessica ordered. "They're going to die here if you don't get them something."

"I'm trying!"

Not hard enough, Jessica thought miserably. She noticed that one of the fish wasn't squirming. Was it dead already? They were *all* going to be dead in a minute or two.

Not knowing what else to do, Jessica bent down and scooped the fish into her cupped hands, cutting her pinkie on a piece of glass in the process. She started toward the kitchen with the fish, but then remembered the bathroom. *There's water in there*, she thought. *Thank goodness Elizabeth left the door open!* She hurried across the hall and dropped the fish into the toilet with a plop.

*   *   *

"The fish are *where?*" Elizabeth asked, wrinkling her nose. She was holding a large crystal punch bowl she'd taken from the Clarks' china hutch. It wasn't perfect, but it would hold the fish.

"In there," Jessica replied, nodding toward the toilet. She dabbed the small cut on her pinkie with a wad of toilet paper. "I practically cut my own finger off saving their lives!" She sniffed.

Elizabeth winced. "Does it hurt a lot?" she asked with concern.

"Yes, but I'll live," Jessica said bravely.

Elizabeth looked down into the blue water with dismay. "Yuck," she whispered. But the fish didn't seem to mind. All four swam around the toilet bowl as though it were home.

Jessica grabbed the punch bowl. "I'll fill this in the tub," she offered. "While I'm doing that, you can reach into the toilet and grab the fish."

"Me?" Elizabeth asked, wide-eyed. "Why do *I* have to dig them out of the toilet?"

"Because I put them in there," Jessica said, jabbing her thumb to her chest.

"Exactly!" Elizabeth folded her arms across her chest. "*You* put them in there, so *you* can get them out!"

"Elizabeth! I can't believe how selfish you're being. Here I risked my life saving those stupid fish, and you're making a big deal about scooping them out of the toilet!" Jessica threw her hands up in the air.

Elizabeth frowned. She wouldn't exactly say Jessica had "risked her life." But she had to admit that Jessica *had* saved the fish.

She bit her lip. Just because Jessica had saved the fish, did that mean *she* had to put her hands in the toilet?

"I *would* fish them out if it weren't for this huge cut I have on my finger," Jessica went on, thrusting her finger in Elizabeth's face. "But I can't go sticking my hands in the toilet. I could get a deadly infection!"

"OK, OK," Elizabeth grumbled. Jessica's cut wasn't quite as bad as she was making it sound, but there was no arguing with her. Besides, it really wasn't a good idea to put an open cut like that in the toilet. "Let's go find a net or something to fish them out with," she said diplomatically.

One of those doors in the hallway has to be a closet, Elizabeth thought. *Maybe the Clarks keep fish supplies in there.*

She went out to the hallway with Jessica on her heels. She opened the first door, which was indeed a closet.

"Ugh," Jessica cried. "Have you ever seen such an ugly shirt in your life?" She pulled out a hanger that held an old green and brown army shirt, and something shiny clattered to the floor.

A knife.

As Elizabeth bent to pick it up, her hand froze.

There was blood on the knife.

Three

◇

"It's a fishing knife," Elizabeth blurted. Then, hesitantly, she added, "Isn't it?"

"Sure," Jessica said flatly, her heart pounding a mile a minute. She gazed down at the object that neither one of them wanted to touch. "A fishing knife."

"And that's obviously fish blood on it," Elizabeth went on.

Jessica nodded. "Obviously," she said, forcing a laugh. "I mean, what else could it be? Certainly not . . . *human* blood, right?"

"Certainly not!" Elizabeth shook her head vehemently. "I mean, that's a fishing shirt. And the knife fell out of the pocket, right?"

"Right," Jessica agreed, glancing at the ugly shirt in her hands. *That has to be it*, she reassured herself.

Jessica bent down and carefully picked up the knife, protecting her hand with Mr. Clark's shirt. Then she tossed both the shirt and the knife in the back of the closet.

Elizabeth breathed a sigh of relief. "We were looking for a net or something to get the fish," she recalled.

"Yeah." Jessica cleared her throat. Her eyes scanned the miscellaneous clothing that hung from the rack and the boxes that were stacked against the back wall. She didn't see anything resembling a net. But she did see a pair of black rubber over-shoes on the floor.

"Hey! How about one of these?" she cried, grabbing one of the overshoes.

"Mr. Clark's rain boots?" Elizabeth asked doubt-fully.

"They'll be dry before he gets back," Jessica pointed out. "He'll never know." She paused. "Unless you'd rather get the fish out with your bare hands?"

Elizabeth shivered. "Not really," she admitted.

Jessica handed the boot to her sister and went to fill the punch bowl with water. Then, holding only the very tip of the boot, Elizabeth scooped each fish from the toilet and plunked it into the bowl.

"There," Jessica said, gazing at the four gold-fish that were happily swimming around the

Clarks' punch bowl. The small amount of water from the toilet that had flowed in with the fish gave the bowl a slightly bluish tint. "That wasn't so bad."

"Not for you, maybe," Elizabeth grumbled, flushing the toilet.

"Hey, this is kind of like a magnifying glass," Jessica noticed as she gazed through the crystal punch bowl. Elizabeth's arm looked about three times the size it usually did.

Elizabeth frowned. "Let's just put it away, clean up, and get out of here."

"Fine," Jessica sighed. *Can't we have any fun?* she wondered.

Jessica looked around. "I don't think we should put this bowl back on the shelf, where it could fall again," she said, walking across the hall to the den. "Besides, the Clarks will probably notice right away they're missing a bowl from their china cabinet. I'll just set it on their dining room table. They'll see it there as soon as they get home."

"Good idea." Elizabeth nodded.

As Jessica walked through the kitchen, the bowl of fish in her arms, something on one of the door hinges caught her eye. She gazed at it through the crystal bowl. *Is that a clump of hair?*

Jessica set the bowl on the floor, where it couldn't fall, and noticed something even stranger.

More blood. Three dime-sized dots right there on the kitchen floor.

Jessica's own blood froze. Her hands flew to her cheeks.

"Elizabeth!" she screamed.

"It does look like blood," Elizabeth agreed, leaning over her sister's shoulder. *But why would there be blood on the kitchen floor?* she asked herself. *Right in front of the basement door?*

"Of course it's blood!" Jessica shrieked. "And look up here." She reached up and pulled a couple of strands of hair out of the door hinge. But instead of showing the hair to Elizabeth, Jessica marched into the living room with it. She picked up the portrait of Mr. and Mrs. Clark and held the strands of hair next to it. "It's a perfect match to Mrs. Clark's hair," she declared.

Elizabeth didn't say anything. She just walked slowly over to Jessica and compared the hair in her sister's hand with the woman's in the portrait.

Jessica turned to her sister. "What if something terrible has happened to Mrs. Clark?" she asked, biting her lip.

"Like what?" Elizabeth asked, folding her arms across her chest.

"I don't know." Jessica paced back and forth. Her face was as white as a sheet. "But think about it.

We've found a bloody knife. We've found blood by the basement door. We've found hair stuck in the hinge." She turned to Elizabeth. "And what about that package that came earlier? You said yourself it was weird that Mrs. Clark didn't call to check on a package she was expecting. What if she didn't call because somebody . . . I don't know, *did* something to her?"

Elizabeth couldn't help herself. She burst out laughing. "Listen to yourself, Jess! This isn't some made-for-TV movie. This is *real life*. Who would've 'done something' to our principal's wife?"

Jessica shrugged. "I don't know. A former student who wanted to get back at Mr. Clark? I'm sure he's made a lot of enemies through the years."

"Well, *I'm* sure there's a logical explanation for the blood and the hair," Elizabeth said firmly. "Being alone in this house is just creeping us out. It's making us imagine all sorts of things that aren't true."

Jessica sighed heavily. "Maybe," she admitted, setting the portrait down.

Elizabeth looked around. "I think we're probably done for today," she told her twin. "Why don't we go on home? I bet tomorrow things won't seem quite so creepy."

"You're probably right," Jessica said, forcing a

smile. "In fact, we may even laugh about this when we come back tomorrow."

"We probably will," Elizabeth agreed.

"Elizabeth?" Mrs. Knight called from the open office door. "Could you come here, please?"

It was Wednesday morning. Elizabeth checked her watch. She still had time to get to her locker before the bell rang if this didn't take too long. "Yes, Mrs. Knight?" she said, stepping into the office. She hoped she didn't sound rude.

Mrs. Knight grabbed a pad and pen from her desk and walked over to the counter. "I was just wondering if you could give me the number where Mr. Clark can be reached," she said, her pen poised over her pad of paper. "I know he hired you and Jessica to house-sit for him."

"Um . . . yeah, he did," Elizabeth said, switching her backpack to her other shoulder. "But he didn't give us any number where he could be reached."

"He didn't?" Mrs. Knight's face fell.

"No." Elizabeth shook her head. "Didn't he leave a number with you?"

"I'm afraid not," Mrs. Knight said, setting her pen down on the counter and resting her chin in her hands. "I don't even know where he went. It was all so sudden. So unlike him. Do you know in all the years I've worked here, he's never even taken a sick day, much less left town unexpectedly?"

"Do you suppose there was some sort of emergency in his family or his wife's family?" Elizabeth asked with concern.

Mrs. Knight shook her head. "No, I remember him telling me once that neither he nor his wife has any family. That was one of the things that attracted them to each other."

"How sad," Elizabeth remarked, feeling sorry for Mr. and Mrs. Clark. She couldn't imagine not having her parents or her sister or even her obnoxious older brother around.

Mrs. Knight shrugged. "Well, I guess he'll be back eventually. I'll just have to hold down the fort until then." She smiled ruefully.

"That's strange." Mrs. Knight stared at the receiver in her hand, then set it on its cradle.

Maria Slater looked up from the attendance cards she was filing. As part of her life-skills class, Maria worked in the school office during her free period on Mondays, Wednesdays, and Fridays. "What's strange?"

"Well, I just got off the phone with Lakeview Nursing Home," Mrs. Knight said, blinking her eyes with confusion. "That's where Donna Clark . . . you know, Mr. Clark's wife?"

Maria nodded.

"That's where she works." Mrs. Knight

drummed her red fingernails on her desk. She looked very confused. "I thought maybe they'd have a number there where the Clarks could be reached. But Donna hasn't been to work in three weeks. The person I talked to claimed that Mr. Clark called in one day and said his wife was taking a leave of absence. Just like that." She snapped her fingers.

Maria stared at Mrs. Knight. She didn't know what to say. "But why would Mrs. Clark take a leave of absence so suddenly?" she asked, scratching her head.

Mrs. Knight shrugged. "And why would she have Mr. Clark call and tell them she wasn't coming in? Why wouldn't she call herself?"

"There must be some explanation," Maria said reasonably.

"Well, of course there is," Mrs. Knight said firmly. "But what is it?"

The doorbell rang when Jessica and Elizabeth were at the Clarks' house again later that afternoon. "I'll get it!" Jessica yelled to Elizabeth. She was in the living room and Elizabeth was in the bathroom.

She opened the door to a boy who was about her age. He had blond curly hair and a splash of freckles across his nose. "Well, hello," Jessica said, tossing her hair over her shoulder with a grin. "Who are you?"

The boy cleared his throat. "I'm David Jeffries," he said. "The paperboy. I'm here to collect. Actually, I'm here to collect for *two* months, not just one."

"*Two* months?" Jessica repeated. She never would have guessed Mr. Clark was the kind of person who didn't pay his bills on time.

"Well, I stopped by last month to collect, but when I heard the yelling, well, I was too embarrassed to ring the bell," David explained.

"Really?" Jessica leaned against the doorjamb with interest. "You heard Mr. and Mrs. Clark yelling?"

"Who's that at the door?" Elizabeth asked, joining Jessica.

"The paperboy," Jessica told her sister. "I can take care of it, Lizzie." She wanted to hear more about the Clarks' yelling at each other.

Elizabeth opened the screen door. "The Clarks aren't here," she told the boy apologetically. "And I don't know when they'll be back."

"Oh." David grinned, exposing a mouthful of metal. "Well, that's OK. I'll just come back tomorrow." He turned to walk away.

"No, you don't understand," Jessica called after him, not wanting him to leave. "The Clarks won't be here tomorrow either. They're, like . . . gone. Now, about this yelling you heard—"

David stopped in his tracks. "What do you

mean, they're gone?" he asked, turning back to the twins. "They're out of town?"

"Yes!" Jessica said impatiently. "Nobody knows when they'll be back."

"That's weird." David looked puzzled. "I wonder why they didn't cancel the paper before they left. They always cancel when they're just going to be away for a weekend. In fact, they usually call about a month ahead of time. They seem like the kind of people who take care of everything way in advance."

Jessica and Elizabeth exchanged looks.

"Well, I guess I'll come back next month," David said, turning to leave again.

"Wait!" Jessica called after him. "What were the Clarks fighting about?"

"Jessica!" Elizabeth nudged her and glared at her sharply. "That isn't our business."

"Well, I couldn't really make out what they were saying," David offered. "They were just yelling. You know, like people do sometimes when they're mad." He paused. "Is it OK if I go now?"

"Sure, whatever," Jessica said, closing the door. She turned to her sister, her brow wrinkled in confusion. "There are just more and more pieces here that don't add up," she murmured.

"I know, but—," Elizabeth began.

Jessica rolled her eyes. "There's got to be a logical explanation," she finished in unison with her twin. But to herself she added, *I wonder. . . .*

Four

◇

Jessica couldn't take it anymore. She had to look around. She had to find out whether there was some sort of explanation for the Clarks' sudden departure. So while Elizabeth was busy watering the plants, Jessica tiptoed up the stairs.

All of the doors in the upstairs hallway were closed, but Jessica guessed the one at the end of the hall was Mr. and Mrs. Clark's bedroom. She put her hand on the knob and slowly turned it.

"Whoa!" Jessica gasped, pushing the door open. "This room is even messier than mine!"

Dresser drawers hung open and clothes were scattered all over the floor, bed, and rocking chair. Underneath all the clothes, Jessica could tell the bed wasn't even made. *Boy, the Clarks sure are slobs!* Jessica thought. *That, or they really left in a hurry.*

Jessica went over to the dresser and fingered the glass figurines. Where *were* the Clarks? Why would they go away and not tell anyone where they were going?

She pulled out one of the drawers that were already partially open. It was empty, so she closed it and pulled out another one. This one was full of women's underwear. Obviously Mrs. Clark's stuff. *Boring,* Jessica decided.

Jessica went to the walk-in closet and flipped the light switch. *Wow,* she breathed, stepping into the closet. *Look at all these clothes.*

There were lots of white nurse's uniforms, but beyond them were tons of other outfits. Dresses, pants, blouses, some casual, some dressy—Mrs. Clark obviously loved clothes as much as Jessica did.

Jessica pulled out a gorgeous purple dress with a long slit. "This would look so great on me," she said, taking it to the full-length mirror that hung on the inside of the closet door. She held the dress up in front of her and admired herself. If only Mrs. Clark would let her borrow it sometime.

Jessica could see herself showing up at a party in a dress like this. Lila and the other Unicorns would be so jealous.

I wonder what else Mrs. Clark has, Jessica mused, returning to the long rack of clothing. But as she did, something about the other side of the closet caught her eye.

It was empty!

Jessica carefully hung the purple dress back where she'd found it. All of the clothes on this side of the closet were women's clothes—Mrs. Clark's clothes. But where were Mr. Clark's clothes?

He probably had *some* of his clothes with him, Jessica reasoned, wherever he was. But he couldn't have *all* of them. Even Mr. Clark had to have more than two or three outfits.

Jessica glanced at all the clothing on the floor. Again, it was all women's clothing. Not men's.

She went back to the dresser and opened all the drawers. Women's T-shirts. Women's underwear. Women's blue jeans. All the other drawers were empty.

"This is so weird," Jessica whispered, perching on the edge of the Clarks' huge, unmade bed. *It's like Mr. Clark not only left town, but he has no intention of ever coming back.*

Rrrring! The noise from the telephone made Jessica jump.

"Can you get that, Jess?" Elizabeth called from downstairs.

"Sure," Jessica muttered, patting her chest to calm her pounding heart. She reached for the cordless phone that was sitting on a table beside the bed. "Clark residence," she said formally.

"Yeah, let me talk to Mr. Clark," a gruff voice demanded.

"Uh . . . he's not here right now," Jessica replied. "Could I take a message?" She looked frantically around for something to write with and something to write on, but she didn't see anything.

"Tell him this is Harry, returning his call. Tell him I'm willing to do the, uh, *work* he asked about." Jessica thought Harry put a weird emphasis on the word *work*.

"Well, Harry," Jessica said, not knowing what else to call him, since he hadn't offered a last name, "I'll give him the message, but I don't know when he'll get back to you. You see, he's out of town—"

"Out of town!" Harry bellowed. He coughed. "He can't be out of town. I just talked to him on Monday."

"I'm sorry," Jessica told him. "But he is."

Harry sighed heavily. He seemed really upset that Mr. Clark was gone. "Well, do you know when he'll be back?" he barked.

Jessica glanced at the closet that was half empty and at the dresser drawers that were *completely* empty. *Maybe never,* she almost said. But she caught herself just in time. "I don't know," she said, running a hand nervously through her hair.

Harry sighed again. "Well, Mr. Clark knows how important this work is. It's gotta be dealt with right away," he said, clearing his throat. "How about I just come over there on Friday at about four o'clock? Will somebody be there to let me in?"

Jessica wasn't sure whether they should be letting a complete stranger into Mr. Clark's house when he wasn't here. On the other hand, if it was something Mr. Clark really wanted done . . .

"What kind of work will you be doing?" she asked, switching the receiver to her other ear.

"Just some stuff in the basement," Harry said mysteriously.

"The basement?" Jessica sucked in her breath.

"Yeah. It won't take very long."

"Well, Mr. Clark said he didn't want anyone to go down in the basement." Jessica chewed her thumbnail.

Harry let out a short laugh. "I'm sure he did. Listen, I know what I'm doing. And believe me, Mr. Clark will rest easier once he knows I've taken care of his little problem."

What little problem? Jessica wondered. *What's down in the basement?*

"So will someone be there to let me in on Friday or not?" Harry wanted to know.

"Uh . . . yeah," Jessica said distractedly. "Someone will be here."

"Good. Mr. Clark will be . . . very pleased," Harry said. Then he coughed again.

He will, huh? Jessica thought. *Well, we'll just see about that.*

"That's ridiculous!" Elizabeth laughed. She had just finished watering the plants and was pouring the remaining water into the kitchen sink.

Jessica grabbed the watering can from Elizabeth's hand and plopped it on the counter. "Is it?" she challenged, her eyes flashing. "Here are the facts." She started counting off on her fingers. "Mr. Clark's side of the closet is empty. Mrs. Clark's side is full. The room looks like Mr. Clark left in a hurry. Nobody seemed to know either one was leaving. Nobody has a number where they can be reached. The paperboy heard them having an argument. There's a bloody knife in a closet. There's a clump of hair on the hinge of the basement door. There's blood on the floor in front of the door. And we're not supposed to go into the basement! I'm telling you, Elizabeth, something's not right here. And don't tell me there's a logical explanation for it all." Jessica paced back and forth like a caged animal.

"But—," Elizabeth started to protest.

"It's obvious Mr. Clark has murdered his wife

and now he's on the run!" Jessica declared fiercely.

Elizabeth's jaw dropped open. She had to admit there were an awful lot of questions here. *But murder isn't the answer to those questions,* she told herself.

"Mr. Clark is just not the type to murder his wife," Elizabeth explained patiently.

Jessica hoisted herself up on the counter. "That's what they always say when they interview the neighbors of the victim," she said grimly.

"You've been watching too much TV," Elizabeth muttered.

"Oh, yeah?" Jessica challenged. "Well, there's a simple way to find out for sure what's going on here."

Elizabeth was almost afraid to ask. "How?"

"We have to go in the basement," Jessica said firmly.

"No way!" Elizabeth argued. "Mr. Clark was very serious about that, Jess. We can't go in the basement."

"Elizabeth! We can't *not* go in the basement. Think about poor Mrs. Clark! Maybe she's still alive. Maybe if we can get down there, we can still save her!" She slid down from the counter and strode purposefully to the basement door.

Elizabeth was right on her heels. "Jessica, don't!" she cried, reaching out to grab her sister's sweater. "Mr. Clark said not to."

But she was too late. Jessica's hand was already on the doorknob.

"Rats!" Jessica kicked at the door. "It's locked!"

Elizabeth sighed with relief. "Well, I for one am *glad* it's locked!" She grabbed Jessica's shoulders and propelled her toward the front door. "Now let's go!"

Once she and Jessica were both outside, Elizabeth pulled the door closed and locked it. "When this is all over and Mr. *and* Mrs. Clark are back safe and sound, you're going to feel really dumb about this," Elizabeth warned.

"Am I?" Jessica raised an eyebrow. "Or are *you* the one who's going to feel dumb?"

Five

"Wow, Mr. Clark always seemed like such a nice guy." Mandy stared at Jessica with a perplexed expression on her face.

"Definitely not the kind to commit *murder*," Tamara Chase agreed. She looked just as shocked as Mandy did.

It was lunchtime on Thursday, and Jessica had just finished filling the Unicorns in on everything that had happened at the Clarks' since she and Elizabeth had started house-sitting.

Jessica shrugged. What could she say? "Haven't you guys ever heard of crimes of passion?" She popped a grape into her mouth and felt the juice squirt out when she bit into it.

Lila shoved her tray of food to the middle of the table. "I can't eat anymore," she said woefully.

"Not when there's a murderer right here at Sweet Valley Middle School."

"We don't know for sure he's a murderer," Janet pointed out.

"Janet's right," Betsy Gordon piped in. "You may have found the murder weapon, but you haven't found the body."

"Well, when Elizabeth and I are at the Clarks' later this afternoon, I'm going to look around for a key to the basement," Jessica said with determination. "That's where the body is."

"Aren't you afraid to go down there?" Ellen wrinkled her nose.

Now that Ellen mentioned it, Jessica *was* a little nervous. But she put on a brave look and shook her head. "Someone has to go down there," she said boldly. "And right now Lizzie and I are the only ones who can."

"That's very big of you, Jessica." Mandy patted her on the back.

"But what if you get down there and don't find a dead body?" Janet wanted to know. "Then what are you going to do?"

"I'll find the body," Jessica declared fiercely. "I know I will!"

Kimberly shook her head sadly. "I just can't believe it. Mr. Clark is our *principal*."

"Principals commit murder too," Lila said, taking a swallow of milk. "Just last week there was this story on *Unsolved Crimes* about a principal who murdered five of his students and then skipped town. No one's seen him in, like, five years. But he's out there. Somewhere."

Janet's eyes grew large. "He killed his *students?*"

Jessica swallowed hard. "Good thing Mr. Clark decided to kill his wife instead of us."

"I admit there are an awful lot of things that need explaining," Elizabeth told her friends at lunchtime. "But there's got to be a logical explanation. Don't you think?"

Julie Porter just stared at Elizabeth. She didn't say a word.

Neither did Maria Slater.

"I mean, obviously there's *something* in the basement," Elizabeth went on, stirring her soup. "Something Mr. Clark doesn't want us to see. But a dead body?"

"You're right. There's got to be *some* sort of explanation," Julie said weakly, taking a sip of milk from her carton.

"Of course there does." Elizabeth nodded emphatically. She turned to Maria. "Don't you agree?"

Maria bit her lip. "Well . . ." Her eyes shifted from Elizabeth to Julie and back to Elizabeth again. She looked as though she had something on her mind.

"Maria?" Elizabeth cocked her head and looked

at her friend with concern. "What's bothering you?"

Maria blinked. "I don't know," she said, taking a deep breath. "Last week I would've said there definitely has to be another explanation. But now . . ." Her voice trailed off.

"But now what?" Julie prompted her. She put her napkin and silverware on her plate and gave Maria her full attention.

Maria glanced around to make sure no one else was listening. "You guys know I work in the office during third period, right?" she said in a low voice, leaning across the table.

Elizabeth and Julie both nodded.

"You know how you said that it was weird that Mrs. Clark didn't call to check on some package she was obviously expecting?" Maria began.

Elizabeth nodded again, then motioned with her hand for Maria to go on.

"Well, yesterday Mrs. Knight called over to the nursing home where Mrs. Clark works," Maria said slowly. "She was thinking maybe the Clarks left the nursing home a number where they could be reached. But do you know what?" Maria looked at them. "Mrs. Clark hasn't been to work in *three weeks*. Mr. Clark called and told them she was taking a leave of absence. Just like that. No one there has heard from her since."

"You're kidding!" Elizabeth's stomach felt hollow.

"So . . . where has Mrs. Clark been these last three weeks?" Julie asked.

"That's a very good question," Maria said, fixing Elizabeth with a serious look.

Bruce Patman looked at Caroline Pearce as though she were crazy.

"It's true!" Caroline hugged her books to her chest. "Mr. Clark killed his wife and now he's on the run."

"Right," Bruce snorted, then turned to walk away.

He knew that Caroline Pearce was the biggest gossip at Sweet Valley Middle School. Telling her something was like posting it on a billboard. The only trouble was that hardly anything she ever said was a hundred percent accurate.

"No, really," Caroline insisted. She had to take two steps to every one of Bruce's to keep up with him, but Bruce didn't care. He simply wasn't interested.

"I heard it from a *very* reliable source," she assured him. Her green eyes twinkled mysteriously.

Bruce glanced at her as they turned a corner. "Who? Jessica Wakefield?" He snorted. He and some of the guys had been sitting at the table next to Jessica's during lunch. They'd all overheard Jessica telling the Unicorns some bizarre story about Mr. Clark's killing his wife—the most bizarre part being the fact that so many of the Unicorns actually seemed to believe her.

But Bruce was a Patman. The Patmans were one of the wealthiest families in Sweet Valley. Not to mention one of the smartest. Bruce wasn't as easily fooled as everyone else.

"It wasn't Jessica," Caroline informed him, stopping in the middle of the hallway.

Bruce turned. "No?" he asked, trying not to appear too interested. "Well, then, who was it?"

Caroline rocked back and forth from her heels to her toes and smirked. "Elizabeth."

"*Elizabeth?*" Bruce stared at her. "Elizabeth *Wakefield?*"

Caroline nodded, hugging her books even tighter.

Bruce ran his hand through his dark hair. *Whoa,* he thought. *That puts a different light on things.*

Everyone knew Jessica Wakefield had a tendency to go off the deep end. You couldn't put much more faith in something she told you than you could in something that Caroline told you.

But Elizabeth was another story.

She was one of the most boring people Bruce knew, but she was *smart.* When she said something, it was usually true.

But Mr. Clark killing his wife? That just seemed so far-fetched. Even if it did come from Elizabeth.

"I heard Elizabeth and Julie and Maria talking during lunch," Caroline said, gazing at her nails.

"What did they say?" Bruce wanted to know.

Caroline shrugged. "Just that Mrs. Clark has been missing for three whole weeks already." She leaned against a locker and twisted her long red hair around her finger. "No one's seen or heard from her in all that time. And now Mr. Clark is missing too." She clucked her tongue. "It doesn't look good for Mr. Clark."

"No, I guess it doesn't," Bruce said, rubbing his chin.

"There has to be a key here somewhere," Jessica muttered to herself as she rooted through a silverware drawer at the Clarks' house later that afternoon.

The door leading to the basement is in the kitchen, so isn't it only logical that the key to the door would also be somewhere in the kitchen? Jessica asked herself.

She sighed. Logic or no logic, the key wasn't in the silverware drawer. She slammed that drawer closed and tried the next one. But all that was in there was a jumble of spoons, spatulas, and a cheese grater.

The drawer below that contained washcloths. And the bottom drawer held dish towels.

There was one more drawer over by the phone. She pulled it open. *Aha!* she thought, her heart racing, as she picked up a blue key.

But when she turned the key over, her heart sank. Attached to the key was a small piece of tape that read Spare House Key.

Jessica tapped the key against her chin and stared at the locked basement door. There had to be a way to get down there. There just *had* to be!

"Don't even think about it, Jess," Elizabeth warned as she wandered into the room with a handful of mail.

Jessica jumped. Was she losing her mind? Had she spoken out loud?

"I know what you're thinking," Elizabeth said, shaking her finger. "You're trying to figure out a way to get into the basement."

Jessica slipped the key into her jeans pocket and followed Elizabeth over to the counter. "We could put an end to this whole thing if only we could get down there," she grumbled.

"We'll put an end to it when Mr. Clark gets back," Elizabeth said reasonably. She put her hand on her sister's back and steered her away from the basement door. "Now come on. We're done here for today. Let's go home."

"I would think you, of all people, would care that a crime has been committed here," Jessica muttered. "I would think you'd want to see that justice was done. Isn't that what your hero Christine What's-her-name would do?"

"Christine *Davenport*," Elizabeth responded

automatically. "And Christine would make sure she had all the facts before jumping to conclusions."

"We *have* all the facts!" Jessica spat, pounding her fist on the counter. "The only thing we don't have is the dead body. And I'm telling you, Elizabeth, that's in the basement."

Elizabeth frowned. "We don't know that."

"We would if you'd help me find a way to get into the basement. You just don't want to know the truth. You can't face the fact that Mr. Clark is a murderer!"

Elizabeth rolled her eyes. "You're being ridiculous," she said, folding her arms across her chest.

No, I'm not, Jessica thought. She was right about this. She *knew* she was.

Mr. Clark had murdered his wife. And one way or another, she was going to prove it.

Six

◇

There has to be a logical explanation for all of this, Elizabeth told herself as she lay in bed that night waiting for sleep to come. *There has to be.*

But what?

She pulled her blanket up to her chin and remembered the conversation she'd had with Mr. Clark. He'd been in such a hurry that he'd hardly even remembered to give her a key. But he *had* remembered to tell her not to go in the basement. *Even though it's locked,* she thought.

Why would he make a point of telling her not to go in the basement when it was locked anyway? What was down there that he didn't want anyone to know about?

A shiver ran through her. *Could Jessica possibly be right?* Elizabeth hated to admit it, but if Mr. Clark *had* killed his wife, it would explain a lot of things. Such as why Mrs. Clark had disappeared three weeks before Mr. Clark did. And why no one knew where the Clarks were or when they'd be back. Even the hair in the basement-door hinge, the knife, and the blood.

But if Mr. Clark had murdered his wife and hidden her body in the basement, why would he have hired Jessica and her to house-sit?

Elizabeth bolted upright in bed. *To throw everyone off the track, that's why!*

The same thing had happened in Amanda Howard's *Murder the Old-Fashioned Way*. In that book, Mr. Wyatt had murdered his wife and buried her in the crawl space under his stairs. Then he left town. But he hired someone to come by and look after his place while he was away. *That way it looked like he was coming back,* Elizabeth realized. But with each day that went by, he got farther and farther away.

What if Mr. Clark wasn't planning to come back? What if he really had killed his wife, and each day that Elizabeth and Jessica went to his house as though everything were OK, he got a little farther away from Sweet Valley?

But if Jessica is right, there should be other clues.

Elizabeth threw off her covers and grabbed a pair of jeans. She was going over to Mr. Clark's house. Now. Before she changed her mind.

* * *

It's dark *at twelve-oh-five in the morning*, Elizabeth realized as she pulled her sweater tighter around her. *Really dark*. Wandering around in the middle of the night wasn't something she normally did, but Jessica was talking about *murder*. Elizabeth just had to find out the truth.

She carried a flashlight, but she didn't want to use it until she got to the Clarks'. She'd need it there so she wouldn't have to turn on any lights and arouse suspicion in any of the neighbors. And she didn't want to wear down the batteries before she got there.

A full moon shone through the trees. The only sound Elizabeth heard was the steady *slap-slap* of her tennis shoes against the sidewalk as she walked along quiet Hampton Drive.

Screeeeech! went a bird—or *something*—in the tree behind her.

Elizabeth jumped. Maybe she should've woken Jessica and asked her to come along. The darkness wouldn't be quite so scary if she wasn't all alone.

No, she decided, she'd been right not to tell Jessica. If she even *hinted* to her sister that she might be right about Mr. Clark, Jessica would have the FBI come in and break down the basement door. And Elizabeth wasn't sure that Jessica was right.

She patted the key in her pocket and kept on walking. *I'll just check out the rest of the house,* she told herself. She'd read enough Amanda Howard books to know that criminals *always* left clues. She just hoped she'd be able to recognize the clues when she saw them.

Elizabeth heard a rustling noise behind her. *What was that?* she wondered, whirling around. Her heart pounded in her throat. A gentle breeze rippled through her long blond hair, and she heard the rustling noise again.

It was just the wind, she scolded herself.

University Avenue was up ahead. And from University she'd turn onto Mercury Drive, the Clarks' street.

Elizabeth stopped. She was at the corner of Hampton and Willow. Maria Slater lived just two houses down Willow Street. She could continue on toward brightly lit University Avenue by herself. Or . . . she could go see if Maria would come with her.

Elizabeth turned and sprinted up the street toward Maria's house.

Maria's house was totally dark. So were most of the houses around it. "Well, what do I expect at twelve-fifteen in the morning?" Elizabeth muttered.

A streetlight illuminated a planter on Maria's

front porch. Elizabeth went to the planter and grabbed a handful of decorative pebbles. Then, taking a deep breath, she walked around to the back of the house.

Maria's window was the one on the corner.

Elizabeth picked up a single pebble and aimed it at Maria's window. It hit the glass with a *plink*. The sound was louder than Elizabeth expected.

She glanced warily from side to side. Had anybody else heard it?

Probably not. In fact, it was possible that even Maria hadn't heard it.

Elizabeth tossed another pebble.

Plink!

And another.

Plink!

Elizabeth hoped Maria's parents wouldn't hear the noise and wake up. "Come on, Maria," she whispered, her eyes glued to the window. "Wake up!"

She tossed one more pebble.

Finally she saw the curtain part a little. "Maria, it's me!" Elizabeth hissed, waving her arms.

Maria opened her window and stuck her head out. "Elizabeth?" she said, blinking with surprise.

"I need to talk to you," Elizabeth said softly, cupping her hands around her mouth. "Can you come down?"

"I guess so," Maria responded. "Wait right there."

"So you think Jessica could be right?" Maria's brown eyes were wide with surprise. She was wearing a pair of pink sweatpants and a pink sweatshirt over her pajamas.

The girls were on their way to the Clarks' house. As they walked, Elizabeth had told Maria everything she'd been thinking.

Elizabeth shrugged. "I don't know what to think," she responded as they turned onto Mercury Drive. "But what you said at lunch today about Mr. Clark's calling up the nursing home where Mrs. Clark works and telling them she was taking a leave of absence got me thinking. If Mr. Clark *did* kill his wife, it's possible no one would find out for a very long time."

"And that's what he would want," Maria said ominously.

Elizabeth stopped walking. "That's his house." She pointed.

Maria looked. "Wow. You wouldn't think he'd commit murder right next door to a church, would you?"

Before Elizabeth could answer, a pair of red taillights blinked on. They belonged to a car that was parked right in front of Mr. Clark's house.

Elizabeth's heart leaped into her throat. "Who could that be?" she wondered out loud as the vehicle roared to life.

"A neighbor?" Maria suggested.

"Look! They're turning around!" Elizabeth gasped as the car swung around in a U-turn. She tugged at Maria's sleeve. "We've got to hide."

The girls darted behind a bush and watched as the car sped past them and around the corner. Elizabeth didn't feel any better once it was gone. Her whole body trembled. "Wh-Wh-Where would they be going at twelve-thirty in the morning?" she stammered.

"Maybe they work the night shift somewhere?" Maria offered.

"Maybe," Elizabeth repeated. Maybe it *was* just a neighbor. And maybe the neighbor often parked in front of the Clarks' house. After all, she had never noticed before whether a car was parked there or not. And maybe whoever the person was, he *did* work the night shift.

Elizabeth peered around the bush. Whoever he was, he was definitely gone now. The street was deserted.

"Well?" Maria looked at Elizabeth. "Are we going over there or not?"

"Yes, we are," Elizabeth replied firmly, rising to her feet.

She and Maria crossed the street and looked up at the house. It was really dark and spooky-looking in the middle of the night. The streetlights cast eerie shadows against the house. Somewhere in the distance a dog barked.

"Hey, did you see that?" Maria grabbed Elizabeth's arm.

"What?" Elizabeth asked.

"Up there!" Maria pointed at a bedroom window.

Elizabeth looked. "I don't see anything," she said carefully.

"Neither do I—*right now*." Maria frowned. "But I swear that two seconds ago I saw a beam of light move across that window."

Elizabeth stared up at the window. It was totally dark. "You must've imagined it," she said quietly, almost in a whisper.

"Yeah, maybe," Maria said, sounding unconvinced. She rubbed her arms. "Being out here in the middle of the night is kind of creepy, isn't it?"

"Yeah, it is," Elizabeth agreed. She reached for Maria's hand. "Thanks for coming with me."

Maria smiled. "You're welcome."

Elizabeth took a deep breath and reached into her pocket for the key. It felt cold against her bare hand.

The girls walked slowly up the wide steps out front. Elizabeth's heart thumped twice for every step she took. "Do you really think this is a good idea?" she asked, stopping halfway up the steps. "Going inside, I mean."

"Well," Maria said, gazing thoughtfully up at

the house, "that's what we're here for, isn't it?"

"Yeah," Elizabeth confirmed. "I just feel sort of funny. I mean, what if we don't find anything? Won't we feel stupid breaking into Mr. Clark's for nothing?"

Maria bit her lip. "But what if we *do* find something?" she countered.

Elizabeth sighed. *Christine Davenport wouldn't hesitate to go inside. Her primary concern is to find out the truth. She doesn't waste time worrying about whether she's right or wrong. She'd charge inside and find out.*

"OK," she said finally, taking her key out. "We're going in."

"Have you been in any of these rooms up here?" Maria whispered as they made their way up the stairs to the second floor. Elizabeth's flashlight lit their way.

"Jessica snooped around in Mr. and Mrs. Clark's bedroom the other day, but I haven't been up here at all," Elizabeth whispered back.

She raised her flashlight and shone it down the hallway. There were two closed doors on each side of the hall and another door at the end of the hall.

"Why don't we just start here and work our way all around the floor?" Elizabeth suggested, turning toward the right.

"Fine with me," Maria responded.

The girls tiptoed over to the first door. Elizabeth turned the handle and pushed the door open. The room had a funny odor to it. Almost like paint.

"Weird," she said, shining the flashlight around.

"I'll say," Maria agreed. She was standing so close to Elizabeth, their shoulders were touching. "What is this room anyway? A bedroom?"

"I don't know," Elizabeth responded, her eyes traveling around the room.

The walls were bare. The shade was drawn. And all the furniture in the room was covered with sheets. "It looks all closed up," Elizabeth observed. "Like someone isn't planning to come back for a very long time."

"Maybe someone isn't," Maria said grimly.

Elizabeth felt a shiver run through her as she slowly made her way around the room. "What's this over here?" She shone the flashlight on a large object in the middle of the room.

"Let's go see." Maria walked slowly over to the object and gingerly lifted the sheet.

"It's a trunk!" Elizabeth said, dropping to her knees in front of it.

"What do you suppose is inside?" Maria wondered.

Elizabeth noticed a key sticking out of a lock on the front. "There's one way to find out," she said, turning the key.

There was a loud clunk as the lock opened. Both girls jumped.

"Everything sounds so loud in an empty house," Maria said, stifling a giggle.

"Especially in the middle of the night," Elizabeth added. "Come on, let's open it."

She put her hands on one end of the lid. Maria put her hands on the other end. And with a steady *cre-e-ak*, they lifted the lid.

Elizabeth shone her flashlight inside. "It's just more sheets," she said, disappointed.

Maria reached in. "Feels like sheets all the way down to the bottom," she announced.

Elizabeth sighed, sinking to the floor. "Well, it's not like I expected to find a letter in here that said, 'I, Mr. Clark, killed my wife and hid the body in the basement.'"

"Just what *are* we hoping to find?" Maria looked at her.

"I don't know," Elizabeth answered, biting her thumbnail. "Just . . . something that'll answer all these questions I have." She grabbed the edge of the open trunk and pulled herself to her feet. "Come on," she said to Maria. "Let's try the next room."

Maria moaned, but she rose and followed Elizabeth.

Elizabeth shone her flashlight on the doorknob, then reached out to turn it. But before she could turn it, she felt someone else turning it—*from the other side of the door.*

Seven

◇

"Aaaaaah!" Elizabeth screamed as a light shone on her face, blinding her.

"Aaaaaah!" screamed another voice.

"What in the world?" someone cried.

Elizabeth raised her hand to shield her eyes from the glow of the flashlight. *"Jessica?"* she cried, squinting at the figure in the doorway.

"Lizzie?" Jessica said with surprise. The beam of the flashlight swept to Elizabeth's right. "And Maria!"

"And Mandy!" Mandy giggled, squeezing in beside Jessica.

Elizabeth took a deep breath and sighed with relief.

"Well, now that we all know each other . . . ," Maria joked, leaning against the wall.

"What are you guys doing here?" Jessica demanded.

Elizabeth folded her arms across her chest. "I could ask you guys the same question," she said, narrowing her eyes at her twin. "How did you get in here anyway? I'm the only one who has the key."

Jessica reached into her pocket and pulled out a blue key that looked exactly like Elizabeth's. "I found it in the kitchen this afternoon," she said, grinning triumphantly. "I had a feeling it might come in handy."

"We were going to check things out tonight and decide whether we wanted to call the police in the morning," Mandy explained. She slapped Jessica's arm. "I *told* you I heard something in the next room!"

"And I told you I saw a light in the window," Maria told Elizabeth.

"So did you guys find anything in there?" Jessica asked eagerly. "That's the only room we haven't been in."

"The only room besides the basement," Mandy chimed in.

Just hearing the word *basement* made Elizabeth's hair stand on end.

"There wasn't anything in there," Maria informed them. "Just a trunk full of sheets."

"*Everything* was covered with sheets," Elizabeth added.

Rrrring!

"Aaaaaah!" they all screamed again.

"What was that?" Elizabeth asked, her heart pounding like a sledgehammer.

Rrrring!

"It's the telephone. Duh!" Mandy said, rolling her eyes.

"But why would the telephone be ringing here in the middle of the night?" Jessica asked in a low voice.

"Especially when no one's even home," Elizabeth added, reaching for her sister's hand. It felt cold and clammy.

Rrrring!

Elizabeth hardly dared to breathe. All four of them stood as still as statues through two more rings. Then an answering machine picked up in the room at the end of the hall.

"Hello," came Mr. Clark's recorded voice. "You have reached the Clark residence. We can't come to the phone right now, but if you'll leave your name and number, we'll get back to you as soon as possible."

"*Maybe* we'll get back to you," Jessica whispered.

Elizabeth swallowed hard. Would there be a message?

"Hello?" said a strange voice with a heavy accent. "You Mr. Clark? . . . This . . . Guo Li. I call from Beijing—"

"Beijing!" Mandy exclaimed.

"Shhh!" the others hissed.

"I have . . ." He seemed to be searching for the right word. "Wallet. I find . . . wallet on train. I . . . send wallet to American . . . Embassy in China, OK? OK . . . good-bye."

Elizabeth's eyes were glazed. "What is Mr. Clark doing in China?" she asked in a confused voice.

"*Now* do you believe me?" Jessica demanded, tapping her foot. "Mr. Clark killed his wife and skipped the country." *Honestly!* she thought. *Some people have to be bitten in the butt with the truth before they finally believe it.*

The four were sitting in a circle in the middle of the kitchen floor. The two flashlights shone on the ceiling above them. *It's just like when we have a séance during a sleepover,* Jessica thought. Only she wouldn't want to try to contact a dead spirit here. Not in this house. She'd be too afraid they'd get a reply.

"But how could he just up and go to China like that?" Maria wanted to know. "It takes time to get shots, a passport, and whatever else you need to go to a place that far away."

"Well, that explains why he waited three weeks to go," Jessica said matter-of-factly. "We all know that Mrs. Clark disappeared three weeks ago.

That's probably when he killed her. And then it took this long for him to get everything else in order so he could escape."

"Ew!" Mandy shivered, hugging her knees to her chest. "Imagine living in this house with a dead body for three weeks."

"Maybe he's been staying in a hotel for the last three weeks," Maria suggested.

"Maybe he has!" Jessica agreed, sitting up a little straighter. "Maybe he's been living it up, ordering room service and watching movies, while his wife lies dead in his own basement."

Elizabeth stretched out her legs in front of her. "So what do we do now?" she asked.

Jessica's eyes shifted to the basement door. She suddenly wasn't in quite such a hurry to go down there and check things out—now that she knew for sure what was there.

"I guess we call the police," Mandy said, eyeing them nervously.

Elizabeth hesitated. "I don't know."

Jessica rolled her eyes. "You *still* don't believe me?"

"No, I *do* believe you. But I've read enough mystery novels to know that the police are going to want some solid evidence. All we have here is circumstantial evidence."

"So what are you saying, Elizabeth?" Mandy asked, cocking her head.

Elizabeth took a deep breath and gazed at the basement door. "I think we have to find a way to get into the basement. I think we have to find out what's down there before we get the police involved."

"But we already know what's down there," Jessica cried impatiently.

"No, we don't." Elizabeth shook her head. "We have our suspicions, but we don't really know."

Jessica bit her lip. "Well, how are we going to get down there? The basement's locked, remember?"

"Maybe we could come back tomorrow when it's light and take the door off its hinges," Mandy suggested.

Maria wrinkled her nose. "How are we going to do that?"

Mandy shrugged. "With a screwdriver."

"I'd much rather do it during the day than at night," Jessica admitted. *If we have to do it at all*, she added to herself.

And it was beginning to look as though they *would* have to do it. They were the only ones who knew what was down there.

"OK, then," Elizabeth said, rising to her feet. "We'll come back this afternoon and take the door off its hinges."

Jessica took one last look at the basement door

and swallowed hard. For the first time, she was *really* scared.

* * *

"Do you really think we're going to find a dead body in Mr. Clark's basement, Jessica?" Elizabeth whispered.

It was three-thirty in the morning and the twins were back at home. They were both in Jessica's room. Jessica was in bed with the covers pulled up to her chin. Elizabeth sat at the foot of the bed, playing with the fringe on Jessica's afghan.

Jessica took a deep breath, then let it out. "Yeah," she admitted. She looked at Elizabeth. "Don't you?"

Elizabeth nodded miserably. She tucked a strand of hair behind her ear. "It's just . . . I-I-I've never seen a d-d-dead body before," she stammered.

"Neither have I." Jessica bit her lip.

"What do you suppose it's going to look like?" Elizabeth asked, drawing Jessica's afghan around her.

Jessica shrugged. "You're the one who reads all those books about dead people. You tell me."

"I don't read books about dead people," Elizabeth protested. "I read *mysteries*." But she had to admit, most of the mysteries she read involved murder. She loved watching Christine Davenport conduct a murder investigation. The way Amanda Howard wrote, you felt as if you were right in the middle of the action yourself.

But with everything that was going on at the Clarks' house right now, Elizabeth was experiencing more "action" than she liked.

"Well, I don't know about you," Jessica said, adjusting her covers, "but I sure will be glad when tomorrow is over and we can call the police."

"Me too," Elizabeth admitted, yawning. She stood up. She was going to go back to her own room, but she stopped at the door. "We're doing the right thing, aren't we, Jess? Breaking into Mr. Clark's basement, I mean."

Jessica propped up her elbow and rested her head on her hand. "We don't have much choice here, Elizabeth."

Elizabeth nodded. "You're right. I just wish he hadn't done it."

"Me too," Jessica said, sighing heavily. "Me too."

Eight

"Did you guys hear what they're saying over there?" Brian Boyd asked at lunch the next day. He plopped his tray down and nodded toward a table where Bruce Patman, Charlie Cashman, and Jim Sturbridge were sitting. He couldn't have heard them right.

"Yeah. Mr. Clark killed his wife and skipped town," Jerry McAllister responded, his mouth full of Cheez Doodles. "It's old news, man."

Brian sat down. "What do you mean, it's old news?" He stared at Jerry in disbelief. "This is the first I've heard of it."

"I don't know where you've been." Jerry shrugged and reached into his bag for another handful of Cheez Doodles.

"Jessica and Elizabeth Wakefield have been

house-sitting for Mr. Clark while he's been away," Aaron Dallas confirmed. "They're the ones who found the body."

Jerry stopped chewing and stared wide-eyed at Aaron. "I didn't know they'd found the body."

Aaron shrugged. "I *think* they have." He shoveled a forkful of green beans into his mouth.

Aaron and Jessica are sort of boyfriend and girlfriend, Brian recalled. *So he'd know what was going on with her.* "Wow," Brian said, opening his carton of milk. "So it's true, then? I never would've believed it."

"Why not?" Jerry asked, reaching for his can of soda with yellow-orange fingers. "You've spent as much time in Mr. Clark's office as I have, Boyd. You know as well as I do he's got a temper."

"Yeah, Mrs. Clark probably burned the hamburgers one night, and then—*ch-k-k-k-k!*" Aaron slid his finger along his throat. "Mr. Clark let her have it."

Jerry grinned and crushed his empty soda can in his hand. "I'm just glad I didn't mouth off *too* much in his office."

"You and me both," Brian said, stirring his mashed potatoes and gravy. "So what's going to happen now? Who's going to be our new principal?"

"Beats me." Jerry shrugged. "Probably Mr. Edwards."

Mr. Edwards was the vice principal.

"I think most of the grown-ups are keeping this whole thing pretty quiet," Aaron said. "At least until the police find Mr. Clark and he admits the whole thing."

"Yeah, he's probably got a contract or something that says they can't fire him until he admits doing something wrong," Jerry put in. "But for the moment, it looks like we're without a principal!"

Brian grinned. "Cool!"

"I found this in my dad's toolshed," Jessica announced, holding up a screwdriver for all the Unicorns to see.

Lila's eyes were wide. "Wow," she said, pushing her lunch tray to the center of the table. "I can't believe you guys are really going to take Mr. Clark's basement door off its hinges."

"What else are we supposed to do?" Jessica asked, shrugging. "A *crime* has been committed here, Lila. And it's our civic responsibility to see that justice is served."

"Do you guys want to come with us?" Mandy offered, cutting her mystery meat into tiny pieces.

Lila shook her head quickly. "I, uh, have some serious shopping to do after school today."

"Yeah, and I'm going with her," Kimberly spoke up.

"We're *all* going with her," Ellen piped in.

Jessica smirked. "You guys are chicken," she said accusingly.

"No, we're not," Tamara argued. "We just trust you to handle it."

"Yeah, right," Jessica sniffed. She flipped her long blond hair behind her shoulder and bit into her turkey sandwich. *Typical Unicorns,* Jessica thought with disgust. *I'm the only one who can stand to get her hands a little dirty.*

Janet leaned across the table. "You know, *everyone's* talking about this, Jessica," she said in a conspiratorial voice. "Everyone's going to remember just who it was who busted Mr. Clark."

Jessica sat up a little straighter. Janet was right. Everyone *would* remember her part in all this.

Her picture would probably be on the front page of every newspaper in southern California. TV stations would call to schedule interviews. Jessica was going to find herself very busy in the weeks to come.

"This is going to be very good for the Unicorn Club," Janet went on.

The Unicorn Club? Jessica thought indignantly. *No way! This is going to be very good for* me!

"So . . . has anybody here ever actually taken a door off its hinges?" Mandy asked, tapping the screwdriver against her hand.

It was after school and Jessica, Mandy, Elizabeth, and Maria were clustered around the basement door at Mr. Clark's house.

"No, but how hard can it be?" Jessica peered closely at the middle hinge.

"The screws are on the inside, though," Elizabeth observed, crowding in beside Jessica. "How are we going to unscrew it if we can't get at the screws?"

"Look at the top part of the hinge," Mandy said, putting her finger on the round head. "Doesn't it look kind of like a nail? Maybe we can wedge the screwdriver in there and pry it off."

"Or pound it up through the bottom." Maria leaned over and peered up at the bottom of the hinge.

Jessica raised her elbows and frowned when she bumped into Elizabeth with one elbow and Maria with the other. "Well, if you guys would give me a little elbowroom, I'd try it."

Everyone took a few steps back.

Jessica tried to wedge the screwdriver under the pin, but she couldn't. The gap between the pin and the rest of the hinge wasn't big enough. "It won't go in," she said, scrunching up her face.

"Here, let me try," Mandy demanded, holding out her hand.

But before Jessica could hand her the screwdriver, the doorbell rang.

Everyone froze.

"Who could that be?" Elizabeth asked, blinking.

Jessica sighed. "There's only one way to find out." She led the way to the front door.

A large man with a face like a bulldog's peered in at them through the window in the door. He was wearing a pair of blue coveralls that were covered with black stains. The name *Harry* was embroidered in red thread on his right pocket. Jessica opened the door and saw an unmarked black van parked at the curb. She could smell the faint odor of cigarette smoke.

"I think I talked to one of you on the phone the other day," Harry said in a rough voice. He carried a large, dented toolbox in one hand and a two-wheeled dolly in the other. "I'm here to do the work in the basement."

"Oh, yeah." Jessica nodded, remembering the man who had called the day she'd been looking around in the Clarks' bedroom.

Harry opened the screen door without waiting for an invitation and stepped inside, banging his toolbox and dolly on the doorjamb. His steely brown eyes seemed to dare them to stop him.

Elizabeth raised her eyebrow at Jessica, but Jessica just shrugged in response.

"I'll get the job done right away," Harry promised, clearing his throat loudly. He bumped his dolly along the carpet as he made his way to the basement.

The girls trooped along behind him.

"Just stay out of the way and there shouldn't be any danger at all," Harry said, setting his things down in front of the basement door.

Danger? Jessica sucked in her breath.

"Um, excuse me." Elizabeth reached out to tap Harry's shoulder, but she stopped just short of touching him.

Harry turned and grunted at her, then pushed his sand-colored hair out of his eyes. His hair looked as though it hadn't been combed all week.

"The basement's locked," Elizabeth informed him with a slight smile. "How are you going to get down there?"

Harry grunted again, then reached into his pocket and pulled out a key that was as dirty as his fingernails. Jessica wrinkled her nose in disgust.

"Haven't you kids ever heard of a skeleton key?" Harry asked with a smirk.

Mandy slowly shook her head. "What's a skeleton key?" she asked.

"It's a key that opens all kinds of locks." Harry dug a paper mask out of one of his coverall pockets and put it on his face. Then he inserted his key in the lock and opened the door.

The girls all strained to see around him. "Don't

come down here!" Harry warned, raising his index finger and fixing them with a serious look.

"We won't," Maria promised, swallowing hard.

Harry stepped through the doorway and pulled the door closed behind him. Jessica and the others all leaned up against the door and pressed their ears against it. They could hear Harry's dolly *bump-bump-bump*ing its way down the stairs.

"What do you suppose he's going to do down there?" Elizabeth asked with a worried look on her face.

"I don't know," Jessica replied. "When I talked to him on the phone, all he said was, 'I'll come do the *work*.'"

"What work?" Elizabeth wanted to know.

Jessica shrugged. "He didn't say."

By this time Harry had made it all the way down the stairs. Jessica heard him cough, then she heard something that sounded like tools being dropped on a concrete floor.

"Maybe he's an undertaker," Mandy suggested.

"He doesn't look much like an undertaker," Elizabeth said doubtfully.

"No, he looks like a hit man," Maria said in a nervous voice.

Bang! Bang! Bang!

"Aaaaaah!" Jessica jumped, bumping heads with Elizabeth.

"Ow," Elizabeth said, rubbing her head.

"Sorry," Jessica muttered.

They heard tools banging around again and then what sounded like a door being opened and closed.

"What is he doing?" Maria demanded.

"I wish I knew," Elizabeth said, putting her ear against the door again.

"I bet Mr. Clark hired him to dispose of the body," Jessica said matter-of-factly.

"Jessica!" Elizabeth hissed.

"What? Doesn't he look like the kind of guy you'd call if you had a dead body you wanted to get rid of?"

Elizabeth made a face.

"Maybe we should call the police now, while he's still here," Mandy suggested.

"No." Elizabeth shook her head. "We still don't have any proof."

"If Harry's really getting rid of Mrs. Clark's body, the police will be able to catch him in the act," Jessica reasoned. "How much more proof will they need?"

"And if he's just . . . I don't know, fixing some pipes or something down there, we're going to look really stupid for bothering the police," Maria pointed out.

"Not to mention that Harry would probably be a little upset," Elizabeth added. "Do you really want to accuse him of something if we're not absolutely positive he did it?"

Jessica frowned. She had to admit Harry did look like the kind of guy who'd pull a gun on you if you so much as looked at him cross-eyed.

"Elizabeth's right," Mandy spoke up. "I think maybe we should wait and see what Harry does before we call the police."

"Thank you," Elizabeth said.

Jessica kept her ear to the door. The mysterious banging noises continued downstairs. "All right," she said reluctantly. "But if he comes up those stairs with anything that looks even close to a dead body, I'm calling nine-one-one!"

"He's coming!" Elizabeth nudged Jessica. They all moved away from the basement door and pretended to be doing other things in the kitchen.

Jessica and Mandy opened the dishwasher and started unloading dishes. Maria opened the refrigerator and pretended to be looking for something. Elizabeth pored over a cookbook.

Harry had been down in the basement doing who-knew-what for almost two hours. But now Elizabeth could hear something banging up the stairs: one, two, three, four, five, six, seven, eight, nine, ten steps.

Harry coughed, then the basement door banged open. His back was to the girls as he pulled something through the doorway. The dolly. And on the dolly was a huge metal box.

Elizabeth's eyes widened.

The box was obviously very heavy, since Harry was working so hard to pull it. Once he got it through the door, he set the box upright while he squeezed back behind it and locked the basement door.

"There," he said, wiping the sweat from his forehead. "That should take care of it. Don't go down there, though. It, uh, really won't be safe for about twenty-four hours."

Harry tilted the dolly back and pulled it through the kitchen. "Could one of you get the front door for me?" he asked over his shoulder.

Nobody moved.

Everyone looked as stunned and scared as Elizabeth felt.

"Come on, come on," Harry said impatiently. "I haven't got all day."

"Um, OK," Jessica said, springing to life. She went to hold the door.

Elizabeth, Maria, and Mandy followed.

They all stood in the living room and watched as Harry carefully wheeled the box through the doorway. It was so big Elizabeth wondered whether it would fit. But Harry managed to get it through.

"We'll tell Mr. Clark you were here," Jessica

called after him as she joined the other girls in the house.

But Harry didn't respond. He just bumped the dolly down the wide steps and out to his black van. The girls raced to the large living room window to watch.

"You all know what's in that box, don't you?" Jessica asked, biting her thumbnail.

Mandy nodded, her eyes wide with fright. "Mrs. Clark," she whispered.

Elizabeth felt a shiver run through her. *We should've called the police when we had the chance!*

"What are we going to do?" Maria asked frantically. "Should we call the police now?"

Elizabeth watched as Harry set up a ramp outside the back doors of his van and wheeled the box into the van. "There isn't time!" she said desperately. "He'll be gone by the time they get here."

Harry pulled the ramp into the back of the van and then slammed the doors closed.

"Where's he going to take her?" Mandy asked. Her face was completely pale.

"Probably someplace where she won't be found for a long time," Jessica predicted.

Elizabeth's heart pounded against her ribs. "We can't just let him do it!"

"Oh, OK. Why don't you go down and tell him he can't?" Jessica said sarcastically as the van started up.

Elizabeth bit her lip. She wasn't about to go down and tell Harry *anything*.

"What are we going to do?" Maria asked, her voice rising.

And that's when Elizabeth got her great idea.

"There's only one thing to do," she said firmly. "We're going to follow him!"

Nine

"I can't believe we're doing this," Maria said, huffing.

The girls were on their bikes, following the black van. It was three vehicles in front of them.

"I can't believe we're keeping up," Jessica retorted. Her face felt hot. Sweat dotted her back. But she kept on pedaling as hard as she could.

"The only reason we're keeping up is because it takes a while for that van to get going again after it stops at a stoplight," Elizabeth remarked. She stood up on her pedals, trying to keep the van in sight.

"He's turning right at the next intersection," Mandy informed them.

When the girls reached the intersection, they turned too. Now they were on a quiet residential street. There were no other vehicles between them and the van.

As they rode on, the houses grew smaller and farther apart, until pretty soon all they could see ahead of them were a few old warehouses. No more houses.

"Does anybody know where we're headed?" Elizabeth asked worriedly.

"I've never been in this part of town before," Maria responded.

"I say we keep following the van," Jessica said firmly, her eyes glued to the van, which was about a quarter of a mile ahead of them.

"Yeah, we've come too far to turn back now," Mandy agreed.

After they biked past three warehouses, the girls came to a huge open area that was surrounded by a long chain-link fence. There were a few smaller buildings in the distance.

"Look!" Jessica turned to the others. "The van's turning in up there."

"What is this place?" Mandy asked, looking around.

"I don't know," Elizabeth replied. "But there's a sign over there." She pointed to a black-and-white sign that was attached to the fence up ahead.

The girls rode up to the sign and stopped.

"Hazardous-waste dump?" Maria said, reading the sign.

The girls watched as the van drove down a long, narrow drive and stopped outside a brown building. Harry got out of the van and opened the back doors. A man came out of the building and helped him.

"Poor Mrs. Clark," Jessica wailed, pressing her forehead against the chain-link fence. "Nobody'll ever find her in there."

"Look! He's leaving!" Elizabeth cried. The black van was making its way back along the long, narrow driveway.

Jessica drew in her breath. "We'd better get out of here!" she exclaimed, turning her bike around.

They all got on their bikes and started heading back the way they'd come.

"Just act casual," Mandy instructed. "Like we always bike alongside a hazardous-waste dump."

Elizabeth could hear a vehicle coming up behind her, but she forced herself to keep her eyes focused straight ahead. They were beside one of the old warehouses now. In less than a minute they'd be alongside those houses. They could always get help from the people who lived there. *Just a little farther*, she told herself, pedaling harder.

Elizabeth's bike teetered as the black van pulled up beside her. Fear clutched her throat as she realized they hadn't made it to that first house yet.

Harry stuck his head out his open window. "Are

you kids following me?" he barked, narrowing his eyes at them.

Maria pulled to a stop behind Elizabeth. "N-N-No," she sputtered, glancing at Elizabeth.

Something in the corner of her eye caught Elizabeth's attention. On the other side of the street, up a steep, grassy hill, was a white house.

Harry frowned and put his van in park. "Aren't you the same four girls I just saw at the Clark house over on Mercury Drive?"

Jessica and Mandy exchanged nervous glances.

Elizabeth's hands grew clammy. Her neck prickled. She leaned toward Maria and murmured, "If he starts to get out of his van, be ready to drop your bike and run up to that house." She inclined her head toward the house on the hill.

Maria nodded.

"I don't know what kind of game you think you're playing," Harry said in a gruff voice, his hand draped haphazardly over the steering wheel. "But following me out here is a really stupid thing to do!"

Elizabeth heard a click, like a door being opened. She didn't wait around to find out if that was what it was or not. She slipped off her bike and let it clatter to the ground. "Run, you guys!" she yelled.

As fast as they could, the girls all took off across the road and up the hill toward the little white house.

Behind her, Elizabeth heard tires spinning as the van roared to life.

Jessica glanced over her shoulder. "Is he going to drive up the grass?" she cried, pumping her arms even harder.

But the van continued on up the road.

"I think he's leaving!" Mandy panted, slowing down.

Elizabeth patted Mandy's arm as she ran past. "We can't be sure," she huffed.

"Elizabeth's right," Maria agreed. "Let's keep going. We'll have the people who live there call the police!"

"Hello? Hello?" Jessica cried, banging on the front door.

"I don't think anyone's home," Elizabeth said glumly.

"I don't think anyone's *been* home in *years*," Mandy added, gesturing toward the huge spider-web that covered the window. Her shoes clomped across the porch as she made her way to the window and peered inside. "There's nothing in here. No furniture or anything."

Jessica's shoulders sagged. "Great," she said, sitting on the top step. "*Now* what are we going to do?"

The girls glanced down at the deserted road below. "Do you think Harry could be waiting for us somewhere down there?" Elizabeth asked nervously as she sat down beside her twin.

"Probably not," Maria responded. But she didn't sound too confident.

"He could be hiding behind that warehouse," Mandy said, biting her lip.

"Or he could've ditched his van and he could be after us on foot," Jessica declared.

"In which case, we can't stay here," Elizabeth said, rising to her feet. Her eyes were wide with fear. Her face was pale.

"Yeah, we have to get out of here," Maria agreed.

"But where are we going to go?" Mandy asked.

"The police!" Elizabeth wiped her sweaty hands on her jeans. "We have to get to the police."

"But how are we going to do that if Harry is down there waiting for us somewhere?" Jessica asked, casting a worried glance down the hill.

"We have to split up," Elizabeth reasoned.

"Split up?" Jessica, Mandy, and Maria cried in unison.

"It's the only way!" Elizabeth flipped her hair behind her shoulder. "We don't *all* have to split up. We can split into two groups. There's only one of him. And if there are two groups of us, at least one group should be able to make it to the police station."

"And send help for the others," Jessica said ominously.

Maria nodded. "That makes sense." She walked

to the end of the porch and strained to see behind the house. "I think we can go up over that hill and end up down on University Avenue. We can get to the police station that way."

"We can also get there by continuing up this road and ending up on South Lake Starr," Jessica said, brightening.

She wondered where Harry was most likely to be if he was lying in wait for them. She didn't want to send her sister off to face Harry, but she didn't want to run into him herself either.

"Jessica, why don't you and I go over the hill?" Mandy suggested, making the decision for her. "Elizabeth and Maria can continue on to South Lake Starr."

Elizabeth took a deep breath. "And assuming nothing goes wrong, we'll meet at the police station in about fifteen minutes."

"If you see Harry, try to circle back the way we're going," Mandy instructed.

"You guys too," Elizabeth said, reaching for Jessica's hand and looking deep into her eyes. "We don't want to take any chances with him."

"No, we don't," Jessica agreed, squeezing her sister's hand. "He's obviously extremely dangerous."

"Well, come on, then," Mandy said impatiently. "It's starting to get dark."

"Yeah, we don't want to be out alone when it's *really* dark," Maria put in.

Jessica nodded. "Not when a guy like Harry is after us."

"Well, I guess we'll see you guys at the police station," Elizabeth said hesitantly.

"See you at the police station," Jessica repeated, hoping this wouldn't be the last time she ever saw her sister.

"Do you think we should take our bikes?" Elizabeth asked Maria as they gingerly picked their way down the hill.

All four of them had abandoned their bikes at the side of the road when Harry had stopped beside them.

"I don't know," Maria said. "We could get to the police station faster if we biked. But if we walked, we could sneak through backyards if we had to."

"Good point." Elizabeth nodded, her hair bouncing on her back.

"Why don't we make sure our bikes are where we left them?" Maria suggested. "Maybe we could lock them together or something. Then we'll head for the police station."

"OK," Elizabeth agreed. Her eyes darted from left to right, scanning for movement in the nearby trees.

Maria stepped on a twig, and both girls jumped. Maria grabbed Elizabeth's arm.

"I don't know if I've ever been so scared in my entire life," Elizabeth admitted in a shaky voice.

"Me either," Maria said.

They proceeded slowly down the hill, all their senses alert.

"Do you think Jessica and Mandy are OK?" Elizabeth asked worriedly.

Maria turned. "I hope they are," she responded. "But Elizabeth, I think right now we have to be more concerned about ourselves." She nodded toward the road.

Elizabeth looked up and saw a pair of headlights. She clapped her hand to her mouth in terror. "Is it Harry?"

"I don't know," Maria said, wide-eyed.

The vehicle zoomed past and Elizabeth sighed with relief. "It was a truck, not a van."

"Come on." Maria waved her hand as she skipped ahead of Elizabeth. "Let's lock up our bikes and get out of here."

"Even if Harry is looking for us, I don't think he'd try anything around here," Jessica said in a hopeful voice as she and Mandy walked quickly along University Avenue. Cars and trucks whizzed past them.

"I think you're right," Mandy agreed. "This street's too busy."

"And it's too well-lit." Jessica glanced up at one

of the bright streetlights above her, grateful it was there.

"But what about Elizabeth and Maria?" Mandy asked. "That street they're on doesn't get much traffic."

"And it probably doesn't have so many streetlights," Jessica added, swallowing hard. She hated to think of her sister out there all alone.

What if Harry *was* waiting just on the other side of that old warehouse? What if he grabbed Elizabeth, threw her in the back of his van, and drove her back to the hazardous-waste dump? What if he pried open that box where Mrs. Clark was and then dumped Elizabeth in there with Mrs. Clark? Jessica shuddered just thinking about it.

"At least we know where Elizabeth and Maria are," Jessica said, trying to make herself feel better. "If they aren't at the police station already when we get there, we'll demand that they send a police car out immediately. We'll drive along the route they should be walking."

"Good idea." Mandy nodded her approval.

All of a sudden Jessica gasped.

"What?" Mandy asked.

Jessica couldn't speak. All she could do was raise a shaky finger and stare goggle-eyed at the black van that was at the intersection ahead, waiting to turn onto University Avenue.

"Oh, my gosh!" Mandy exclaimed, grabbing Jessica's arm. "Is that Harry?"

"I don't know," Jessica cried. Her heart pulsed in her throat.

Both girls were paralyzed with fright as the van drew closer and closer. But as it passed, Jessica got a look at the driver. "It's a woman driving!" she said, feeling her shoulders relax.

"Good!" Mandy breathed a sigh of relief.

"Come on." Jessica tugged at Mandy's blouse. "The police station isn't far from here."

"Let's run!" Mandy suggested.

"OK," Jessica agreed. The sooner they reached the police station, the better!

Ten

◇

"Elizabeth! You're alive!" Jessica screamed, running toward her sister.

Elizabeth laughed. "So are you!" She threw her arms around Jessica.

They were in front of the Sweet Valley police station. A row of police cars was parked out front.

"We saw a black van, but it wasn't Harry's," Mandy told Elizabeth and Maria.

"I know what you mean," Maria put in. "Every time Elizabeth and I saw headlights, we were sure it was him."

"So, are we ready to go in?" Mandy asked, rubbing her hands together.

Elizabeth glanced over at the one-story brick building. "Yeah," she said. "Let's get this over with."

*   *   *

"You do the talking, Elizabeth," Jessica hissed as Maria pulled open the door to the police station.

"Me? Why me?"

"Because you're the writer," Mandy said. "You always know what to say."

Elizabeth sighed. She knew what to say when it was something about the basketball team's winning a big game or the debate club's going on to the state championships. But when it came to talking to the police, she had no *idea* what to say.

They found themselves in a brightly lit lobby. The walls were painted green, the floor was tiled, and fluorescent lights hung from the ceiling. To the right was a huge glass panel.

Several uniformed police officers milled around on the other side of the glass. One talked on the phone. Two others were looking at some papers.

Elizabeth approached the glass alone, the other girls behind her. But the three officers on the other side continued to go about their business.

Elizabeth cleared her throat.

Still no response.

Finally Jessica stepped forward. "You've got to get their attention, Elizabeth," she said, pounding her fist on the glass.

The officers all turned.

The female officer spoke into a microphone at her desk. Her voice came out over a loudspeaker above the window. "Can I help you girls?"

"We need to speak to someone in charge," Jessica said with authority.

The officers all looked at each other and began talking behind the soundproof glass.

Finally a tall officer with thick dark hair and wire-rimmed glasses walked through the doorway beside the glass partition.

He was so tall Elizabeth had to tip her head back just to read his name tag: Officer Larson. "What can I do for you girls?" he asked.

Jessica nudged Elizabeth.

Elizabeth took a deep breath. "Uh . . . we'd, uh, like to report a, uh, murder," she managed to get out.

"You would, huh?" Officer Larson folded his arms across his gigantic chest and looked at Elizabeth as though she'd said she'd like to report a spaceship landing in her backyard. "And do you know this person who was murdered?"

"Well, not really," Elizabeth admitted. Her stomach swarmed with butterflies. "But we know the murderer. He's our principal. Mr. Clark."

"He lives over on Mercury Drive," Maria put in.

"He killed his wife," Jessica said in a low voice. Her eyes blazed. "And now he's skipped town."

"We have proof," Mandy offered.

"We wouldn't have come without proof," Elizabeth assured him.

Officer Larson's brow wrinkled. His eyes darkened. "Why don't you girls come with me?" he said, leading them down the corridor. "We'll go into my office and you can tell me the whole story from beginning to end, without leaving anything out."

"You're sure about all this?" Officer Larson fixed them each with a serious look.

The girls were sitting around a desk in Officer Larson's small office. They had just finished telling the whole story.

"Positive!" Jessica declared.

"Our bikes are still lying by the road across from the hazardous-waste dump," Maria informed him.

"And if you go right now, you can get that box before the people there do whatever it is they do with hazardous waste," Mandy went on.

"Poor Mrs. Clark," Elizabeth whispered.

Officer Larson frowned. He stood up and reached for his hat. "I think before we check out the dump, we should check out the residence," he said grimly. "You kids better come along."

"Y-Y-You mean in a p-p-police car?" Mandy stammered.

Officer Larson smiled. "That *is* how we get around here in Sweet Valley." He cleared his throat and turned serious again. "I better go talk to the chief. We'll need a warrant. Probably some backup too. I'll be right back." He hurried out of the room.

Jessica glanced at Elizabeth, whose eyes were as wide as her own. *Backup? That means this must be a really dangerous situation*, Jessica thought. *They're probably going to give us medals or something for our bravery. Maybe they'll even honor us at their policemen's ball or whatever.*

Jessica smiled just thinking of it. Lila Fowler would be so jealous if Jessica got to go to a policemen's ball. Even with all of her father's money, Lila wouldn't be able to buy her way into something like that.

But hey, Jessica thought with a shrug, *I'm only doing my civic duty.*

This is just the kind of situation Christine Davenport would be in, Elizabeth thought breathlessly as they sped toward Mr. Clark's house with sirens blaring and lights flashing. There was at least one more police car behind them. Maybe two.

Elizabeth sat in the front seat with Officer Larson, while Jessica, Mandy, and Maria rode in the back, behind a glass partition.

Well, maybe Christine wouldn't actually be speeding to the scene of the crime in a police car, Elizabeth admitted as they zipped past several cars that had pulled over to the right to let them pass. Christine usually got to the scene of the crime by herself. But she always managed to be there when the police were there.

"Don't worry, Elizabeth," Officer Larson said reassuringly. "We'll get to the bottom of this."

Elizabeth swallowed hard. "What are you guys going to do?"

Officer Larson's eyes never left the road. "I think our first plan of attack is to get down in that basement and see what we find."

Elizabeth leaned her head back against the headrest and sighed. *At least this will all be over soon.*

Jessica glanced up absently at Mr. Clark's house as the police car came to a stop at the curb. "Hey!" she said, looking again. "There's a light on in there!"

Mandy leaned toward the window. "Did we leave that on?"

"I don't think so." Maria slowly shook her head. "It was daylight when we were here before. We didn't need any lights."

Elizabeth yanked Jessica's door open and stuck her head inside. "You guys!" she said frantically. "There's a light on!"

"We know," Maria said, stepping out of the car on her side.

"Relax," Officer Larson said, resting a hand on Maria's shoulder. "Why don't you all wait here until we can check the place out?" He motioned to the officers in the car behind theirs and they all ran up the wide steps leading to the house.

Jessica gasped as she saw movement at the living room window. "There's someone in there!" she cried.

"Boy, I'm glad we didn't hang around here," Maria said in a scared voice.

"Me too," Elizabeth chimed in.

"Who do you think is in there?" Jessica asked. "A burglar?"

"Or did Harry come back?" Mandy wondered.

Just then the front door opened. *And out walked Mr. Clark.*

"Mr. Clark!" Elizabeth exclaimed, running up the steps behind the officers. "What are you doing here?" She stared at him in shock.

Mr. Clark was dressed in a pair of jeans and an olive green V-neck shirt. He looked confused. "I think the question is, what are *you* all doing here?" he asked, glancing from Elizabeth to the police officers.

The door opened wider, and a woman stepped up to the door. Jessica drew in her breath. "It's the woman from the picture!" she gasped.

"You mean Mrs. Clark?" Mandy scratched her head.

The woman bent down and picked up a small child with dark eyes and shiny, shoulder-length black hair. The little girl put her thumb in her mouth, then rested her head on the woman's shoulder.

Jessica's jaw dropped. "What is going on here?" she asked, staring wide-eyed at the threesome standing in the doorway.

Officer Larson turned to her. "You tell me."

Eleven

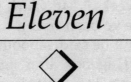

"There was a box," Elizabeth began. She looked from Mr. Clark to Mrs. Clark to the little girl. *Who was that little girl?* she wondered.

"It was a *big* box," Jessica added, spreading her arms wide to show just how big the box was. "We saw Harry bring it up from your basement, Mr. Clark." Her voice was accusing.

Officer Larson cleared his throat. "The girls were a little concerned about what might be *inside* the box," he explained.

The Clarks looked confused.

"I don't know what you're talking about," Mr. Clark said, scratching his head. "What box? And who's Harry?" He looked at his wife.

"You'll have to excuse us if we seem a little flustered," Mrs. Clark told the police officers.

Then she smiled at the little girl, who was playing with a toy telephone at her feet. "We just got home from China, and I'm afraid we're a bit jet-lagged."

"Not to mention overwhelmed by the events of the past few weeks." Mr. Clark joined his wife on the couch. "We've been trying to adopt a child for some time now," he said, smoothing the little girl's hair. "We tried agency after agency, but do you know how long the wait is at some of these places?"

"Five to six years," Mrs. Clark said in a tired voice.

"Five to six *years?*" Maria repeated.

Mrs. Clark nodded. "I didn't think we'd *ever* get a child," she said wistfully. She looked at her husband. "But then we heard about another agency that works with orphanages overseas. They place older children. Children who for one reason or another have lost their homes and their families.

"I got a call from the agency about three weeks ago," Mrs. Clark continued. "They had a child, but if we wanted her, I had to go over to China right away and get the paperwork started."

"You mean you had to drop everything and go?" Elizabeth asked.

"That's the way these things usually work," Mrs. Clark replied.

"And then once it looked like things were definitely going to go through, she called me." Mr. Clark smiled affectionately at his wife and new daughter. "So I caught the next plane to Beijing."

Elizabeth felt a stab of guilt in the pit of her stomach, not to mention embarrassment. They had really jumped to conclusions.

"Well, why didn't you tell anyone where you were going?" Jessica demanded.

Mr. and Mrs. Clark exchanged a look. "We wanted to make sure this was really going to happen before we told people," Mr. Clark explained.

"You see, a couple of years ago we thought we were going to get a baby from Romania," Mrs. Clark added. "But when we got there, things somehow fell through. That was heartbreaking enough. When we got home, however, we had to tell everyone we didn't get a baby after all."

"That was even worse," Mr. Clark said grimly.

Mrs. Clark nodded her agreement. "We didn't want to go through that again," she said, taking her husband's hand. "So we decided this time we wouldn't tell anyone. Not until we actually came home with a child."

"Wow." Elizabeth's eyes grew moist just listening to them talk. *Poor Mrs. Clark. Poor Mr. Clark!* She could hardly imagine what they must have gone through to have a child. "So this little girl is yours?" she asked, getting down on her knees beside the child.

"Yes," Mrs. Clark replied, beaming with pride. "The people in the orphanage didn't have a name for her, so we're going to call her Janelle. It means 'God is gracious.'"

"Hi, Janelle," Elizabeth said, smiling at the little girl.

Janelle kept her head down but raised her eyes to look at Elizabeth. Elizabeth pressed the coin return on the toy telephone, and three toy coins jangled down to a slot at the bottom of the phone. Janelle's whole face lit up with surprise.

"OK," Jessica said, blinking. "I understand all that." She glanced over her shoulder at the basement door. "But then what's in the basement? Why did you make such a big deal about us staying out of there?"

Mr. Clark glanced at his wife and smiled. "Lead paint," he told Jessica in a patient voice.

"Lead paint?" Maria wrinkled her nose.

"This is an old house, girls," Mrs. Clark explained calmly. "Old houses have lead paint. And that can be very hazardous to children, so of course we wanted it all removed. Just in case we *did* get a child."

"The paint removal process creates a lot of dust and debris," Mr. Clark went on. "I didn't want you girls to go down there and breathe it in, any more than I would want my own child to." Suddenly he turned to his wife, as though he'd just remembered something. "Well, I suppose Harry was the man I hired to come in and remove the paint," he said.

Elizabeth nodded. That made sense. "And the box we saw him bring up from the basement was probably full of debris," she reasoned.

"Which explains why he dumped it at the hazardous-waste dump," Mandy put in.

"You mean you girls followed this man out to the hazardous-waste dump?" Mrs. Clark asked incredulously.

Mr. Clark shook his head. "Just what did you think was in that box anyway?"

The twins exchanged a look. Somehow Elizabeth didn't think it was a good idea to tell Mr. Clark exactly *what* they'd thought. "We, uh, didn't know for sure," she fudged. "We thought maybe Harry had stolen some of your stuff." She raised her eyebrows at her sister. "Right, Jess?"

"Huh? Oh, yeah . . . right," Jessica agreed, picking up on Elizabeth's signal. "Since you told us not to go down in the basement, we had no idea what was down there. For all we knew, that was where you kept the family silver or something."

"And since we were the ones who let Harry in, we wouldn't have been able to live with ourselves if it turned out he was a thief," Mandy added.

Elizabeth glanced at the police officers. She hoped they wouldn't give them away.

Officer Larson held back a smile. "Well, it looks like everything is in order here," he said, putting on his hat. "So I guess we'll be going now."

The other officers stood up too. Officer Larson motioned for the girls to follow them.

"I just have one question," Jessica said, tapping her chin thoughtfully as she walked toward the door. "You went to China to bring home a little girl. That explains why Mrs. Clark left three weeks before you did and why you left so suddenly. And you had lead paint in your basement that you wanted to get rid of. That explains why you wanted us to stay out of the basement. But Mr. Clark, I have to tell you I was, uh . . ." She paused for a moment. "I was looking for . . . fish food in your bedroom closet and I happened to notice that Mrs. Clark had a ton of clothes in there, but you didn't have anything. How do you explain that?" She folded her arms across her chest.

"Well, I'd started moving us out of that bedroom and into the room down the hall. We'd been using that extra room as a study, but now that we have a child, we need another bedroom."

Of course! Elizabeth thought, remembering the

room with the trunk. Mr. Clark had been painting in there. That was why it smelled funny and why there were sheets all over everything.

Elizabeth grabbed her sister's arm. "Mr. and Mrs. Clark are obviously tired," she said. *And obviously innocent,* she thought. "We should go."

"Just a minute." Jessica stepped away from Elizabeth. She glanced back toward the kitchen. "Did you know there's some hair stuck in the basement door hinge?" she asked Mr. Clark. "And there's blood on the floor right outside the door!"

"Jessica," Elizabeth said with embarrassment—though she had to admit she was still curious about that blood too.

"I can explain that," Mrs. Clark said, smiling at her husband. "The day I got the call from the agency, I was so excited that I went running across the kitchen, yelling for Jon. And I slipped over by the basement door. I probably caught my hair in the hinge a little bit. And I had a pair of scissors in my hand. I actually cut my leg with them when I fell. It bled a little," she said sheepishly.

"You should never run with scissors," Mandy said, wagging her finger at Mrs. Clark. "They teach us that in, like, first grade."

Elizabeth grinned at Maria.

Jessica ran her hand through her hair. "But there's a knife in your hall closet," she said. She was starting to sound a little desperate now.

"A knife?" Mrs. Clark looked at her husband with surprise.

Mr. Clark shrugged. "I don't know what you're talking about, Jessica."

"I found a knife in your closet," she insisted. "It was in that really ugly jacket. There was blood all over it."

Mrs. Clark nodded knowingly. "I think she's talking about your fishing jacket, dear," she said, slipping her arm through his.

Mr. Clark slapped his hand to his head. "Of course. My fishing jacket." He rolled his eyes. "There *is* a knife in that pocket. I use it for cleaning fish."

"Actually, Jon," Mrs. Clark said, frowning at him, "you're going to have to be better about putting things away now that there's a child in the house. We can't have a toddler playing with a knife."

Mr. Clark sighed. "You're right, dear. I'll take care of it right away."

"I think you girls should stick to house-sitting from now on," the female officer chuckled. "Leave the detective work to us, OK?"

"OK," Elizabeth promised. But after this fiasco, she figured that she and Jessica were probably out of the house-sitting business. She could forget about buying that computer game she wanted.

Maybe Mom and Dad will give it to me for my birthday. "We're really sorry, Mr. Clark," she said sincerely. "I hope you're not angry with us."

"I probably *should* be angry with you girls for dragging the police out here," Mr. Clark said sternly. "But I'm just so happy to be home. So happy to have my little girl." He picked Janelle up and looked at her as though she was the most amazing thing he'd ever seen.

"Come on, girls," Officer Larson said, leading them to the door. "Let's let these people get some rest."

"Will you be back at school on Monday, Mr. Clark?" Maria asked.

"I sure will," Mr. Clark replied, grinning. "And I can't wait!"

"I feel so stupid," Elizabeth groaned as she and Jessica got ready for bed that night.

"So we let our imaginations get away with us." Jessica shrugged. "Big deal. It's not like anyone got hurt or anything." She held her washcloth under the running water, then washed her face.

Elizabeth uncapped the toothpaste and squeezed a blob out onto her toothbrush. "I know," she said with a sigh. "I just feel bad for doubting Mr. Clark."

Jessica snorted. "Give me a break, Elizabeth," she said, drying her face with her towel. "It's the *principal* we're talking about here. It's not like you're really supposed to *trust* him or anything."

Elizabeth raised her eyebrows, then spit her toothpaste into the sink. "Well, actually—"

"Besides, we covered it up pretty well," Jessica went on. She tossed her towel at the hamper, but it missed. *Oh, well,* she thought. She boosted herself up onto the counter. "Telling Mr. Clark that we thought Harry was a thief was a great idea! No one's ever going to know what we really thought."

"Are you sure about that?" Elizabeth asked, replacing her toothbrush in the holder. "What about the kids at school? Everyone was talking about the dead body you and I were supposedly going to dig up in the Clarks' basement today."

Jessica felt her blood grow cold. "I, uh, forgot about the kids at school," she said nervously.

"Well, I haven't," Elizabeth declared. "Everyone at school thinks Mr. Clark killed his wife. It's all anyone's been talking about the last couple of days."

Jessica hated to admit it, but Elizabeth was right. Of course, she'd sworn the Unicorns to secrecy . . . but the Unicorns weren't exactly known for keeping secrets.

Jessica drummed her fingers against her chin and thought for a minute. If each of the Unicorns had told just two other people, and each of *those* people told two other people . . . the possibilities gave her a headache. "People are going to think we're really stupid," Jessica moaned.

"Forget about what people are going to think about *us*," Elizabeth said in a serious voice. "Jessica, think about how people are going to act around *Mr. Clark!* They think he's a murderer!"

Twelve

"We have to tell everyone we were wrong," Elizabeth said sensibly as she and Jessica walked to school on Monday morning.

"No!" Jessica cried. "I mean, we can't say it like *that*." She kicked at a stone in her path as they walked. "Maybe we have to let people know that Mr. Clark didn't kill his wife, but we don't have to make ourselves look so bad in the process."

Elizabeth laughed. "I don't know how we can say it without looking bad."

"Well, we have to find a way," Jessica insisted.

"Hey, Jessica!" Lila waved as the twins crossed the street in front of the school. Her chauffeur had just dropped her off.

Lila adjusted her bag on her shoulder. "So?" she said, glancing expectantly from Jessica to Elizabeth. "What happened when you guys went to Mr. Clark's on Friday? Did you find Mrs. Clark's body?"

"Oh, yeah. We found it, all right," Elizabeth said dryly.

Jessica nudged her. "What Elizabeth means is, uh, well . . ." How could she say it without giving Lila the wrong impression?

"What I mean is . . . Mrs. Clark is *alive*," Elizabeth blurted out.

Lila's jaw dropped. "She is?" Lila looked at Jessica. "You mean when you guys got down to the basement, you saved Mrs. Clark's life?"

"Yeah, that's it!" Jessica nodded eagerly. *Maybe we can still come out of this whole thing looking like heroes.*

"Jessica!" Elizabeth frowned.

But before Jessica could say anything more, she heard Caroline Pearce's voice. "Mr. Clark!" she cried with surprise. "You're back!"

Elizabeth and Jessica ran for the school as fast as they could. Mr. Clark was standing just inside the doorway. Caroline, Bruce Patman, and some other kids were there too. But no one was standing very close to him. Everyone looked a little nervous.

Mr. Clark raised his hand to scratch his head, and Brooke Dennis flinched.

Bruce and Aaron stepped back.

"Aren't you supposed to be in jail or something?" Jerry McAllister said boldly.

"Jail!" Mr. Clark laughed. "Why would I be in jail?"

"Well, Jessica said—"

"I never said anything about jail!" Jessica argued, her hands planted firmly on her hips.

"That's right, Jerry," Elizabeth interrupted, raising a nervous eye to Mr. Clark. "We never used the word *jail* when we talked about Mr. Clark."

Elizabeth racked her brain for something else to say, some explanation they could give to let the other kids know that Mr. Clark hadn't murdered anybody, without letting Mr. Clark know that was what she was doing.

"We may have used the word *mail*," Jessica admitted. "After all, bringing in the mail was one of our jobs."

"Yeah." Elizabeth nodded. "Mr. Clark sure got a lot of *mail* while he was in China."

"China?" Caroline wrinkled her nose.

"Yes, haven't you heard?" Jessica asked sweetly. "Mr. Clark has been in China this past week. He and his wife adopted a little girl. Right, Mr. Clark?"

"Well—," Mr. Clark began, looking sheepish.

"You and your *wife?*" Bruce glanced at the twins. "I thought you guys said—"

"And how is little Janelle?" Elizabeth stepped forward to distract Mr. Clark.

The principal beamed. "She's doing just fine. She slept *under* her bed last night instead of in it, but they warned us at the agency that that might happen."

"You mean your wife is alive?" Caroline's eyes were wide with shock.

Mr. Clark furrowed his brow. "Of course."

"You didn't ki—," Bruce began.

"Isn't it wonderful that Mr. and Mrs. Clark are finally back?" Elizabeth asked everyone. She turned to Mr. Clark and giggled shyly. "Mrs. Clark has been gone so long that some people might even think she'd died or something."

"Yeah, imagine that!" Jessica said, laughing nervously.

Mr. Clark gave a tentative chuckle.

"You know what I think?" Jessica's eyebrows shot up.

"I'm almost afraid to ask," Lila muttered.

Jessica smiled brightly. "I think we should have a party to celebrate Mr. and Mrs. Clark's coming home."

"A *party?*" Lila said, as though she'd never heard the word before.

"Yeah, like a baby shower or something." Elizabeth nodded enthusiastically. "Would you like that, Mr. Clark?"

"We could have it here at school," Jessica went on, her eyes shining. "We'll decorate the gym and have cake and punch."

"And presents for Janelle," Elizabeth put in.

Mr. Clark looked stunned. "I—I don't know what to say. . . ."

"You just leave the details to us," Jessica said, ushering him down the hall. "We'll tell you when and where. But right now I'm sure you have a million things to do."

"I can't believe you actually thought Mr. Clark killed his wife!" Janet scoffed. It was lunchtime and Jessica was having lunch at the Unicorner.

"Really, Jessica." Lila rolled her eyes.

"Hey, I never actually *said* he killed her," Jessica argued, slamming her milk carton down. "All I said was there were some things that didn't quite add up."

"And because there were some things that didn't quite add up, you *assumed* Mr. Clark killed his wife," Tamara accused.

"And you went and told *everyone,*" Kimberly added, pushing her tray to the center of the table.

"Making us look bad," Lila chimed in.

Janet fixed Jessica with a steady look. "Being a Unicorn is a serious responsibility," she informed her. "When one Unicorn does something to make herself look bad, it makes us *all* look bad."

Jessica squirmed in her chair. In her opinion, her friends were blowing this whole thing way out of proportion. "Hey, it's not my fault if everyone thought Mr. Clark killed his wife based on one little thing I might have said." She wiped her chin with her napkin and tried to look cool.

"What you said was, '*Mr. Clark killed his wife,*'" Ellen pointed out.

"I don't think I worded it quite like that." Jessica shook her head. "Besides, you guys are forgetting that I'm the one who found out what *really* happened. And when I did, I told you all."

Janet and Lila exchanged a look.

"I did," Jessica insisted, nibbling a french fry. "And this baby shower we're having for the Clarks? That was my idea." Jessica jammed her thumb to her chest. "The whole school's going to be there, you know. Are you guys going to help me, or do I have to plan this whole thing by myself?"

Mandy looked thoughtful. "I've never been to a baby shower before."

"Neither have I," Belinda Layton put in.

"We could decorate with purple and white streamers," Lila suggested.

"Don't forget balloons," Mandy said, tossing a fry into her mouth.

Jessica felt her shoulders relax. *Now this is more like it.* Planning a party was tons more interesting than analyzing who thought what about Mr. and Mrs. Clark all week.

Thirteen

"Oh! She's so cute!" Lila gushed. It was Friday afternoon and the Clarks were just walking into the gym for their baby shower.

"I didn't think you liked kids, Lila," Jessica said, grinning.

"I like kids!" Lila looked insulted. "As long as they keep their dirty fingers off me." She brushed an imaginary speck of dirt off her blue cashmere sweater.

Mrs. Clark walked over to them with Janelle and smiled. The little girl's arms were wrapped tightly around her mother's neck, but she stared at Jessica and Lila with big brown eyes.

"This is really nice," Mrs. Clark said, gazing up at the purple and white streamers that hung from the ceiling. "Did you girls do all this?"

"We had a little help from the janitor," Jessica admitted.

Mr. Clark came over to join them. "It was really nice of you to plan a baby shower for us," he said, putting his arm around his wife.

"Hey, planning a party is what the Unicorns do best," Lila said with a wave of her hand.

"Wow, it looks like the whole school is here," Elizabeth said, folding her arms across her chest and gazing around the gym.

"I think you mean it *sounds* like the whole school is here," Jessica corrected her. It was so noisy, Jessica could hardly hear herself think.

Mr. and Mrs. Clark were opening their gifts in the middle of the gym, but there were so many people that no one could see what they were opening or hear what they were saying. So some of the kids had broken away in small groups to talk. Another group was playing basketball.

Elizabeth took a sip of her punch. "I'd say the shower is a success, though. Wouldn't you, Jess?"

"Definitely," Jessica agreed.

"Janelle is going to be so spoiled by the time the day is over." Elizabeth grinned.

"No kidding. Look!" Jessica pointed.

Across the gym, Aaron Dallas was giving Janelle a piggyback ride. "That's so cute!" Jessica exclaimed.

"Girls?" Mrs. Whitney called from the kitchen. "Should we bring out the cake yet?" Mrs. Whitney was one of the school cooks.

Elizabeth nodded. "I think this crowd is pretty hungry."

"Do you think Janelle had a good time?" Elizabeth asked Mrs. Clark after the cake had been eaten and the presents had been opened.

"I think she had a wonderful time!" Mrs. Clark smiled. "Thank you so much for all you've done— you and all the kids here at Sweet Valley Middle School. We're so thrilled by this show of support."

"You're welcome." Elizabeth smiled back. "Would you like me to help you gather the presents?"

"That would be very nice." Mrs. Clark began dividing the clothing, linens, and toys into separate piles.

Elizabeth wadded up wrapping paper and stuffed it into one of the two large garbage bags. While she was working, the light reflected off Mrs. Clark's earrings. They were long, silver earrings that twisted in an intricate pattern. Elizabeth couldn't help but admire them.

"Those are really nice earrings," she commented.

Mrs. Clark fingered one. "You think so?" She looked pleased.

"Yes, I do." Elizabeth nodded eagerly. "Where did you buy them?"

Mrs. Clark grinned. "I *didn't* buy them. I made them."

"Really?" Elizabeth asked with interest. "Is making jewelry hard?"

What happens when Elizabeth decides to make some earrings? Find out in Sweet Valley Twins #110, PUMPKIN FEVER.

Bantam Books in the SWEET VALLEY TWINS series.
Ask your bookseller for the books you have missed.

Sweet Valley Twins Super Editions

Sweet Valley Twins Super Chiller Editions

Sweet Valley Twins Magna Editions

SIGN UP FOR THE SWEET VALLEY HIGH® FAN CLUB!

Hey, girls! Get all the gossip on Sweet Valley High's® most popular teenagers when you join our fantastic Fan Club! As a member, you'll get all of this really cool stuff:

- Membership Card with your own personal Fan Club ID number
- A Sweet Valley High® Secret Treasure Box
- Sweet Valley High® Stationery
- Official Fan Club Pencil (for secret note writing!)
- Three Bookmarks
- A "Members Only" Door Hanger
- Two Skeins of J. & P. Coats® Embroidery Floss with flower barrette instruction leaflet
- Two editions of *The Oracle* newsletter
- Plus exclusive Sweet Valley High® product offers, special savings, contests, and much more!

Be the first to find out what Jessica & Elizabeth Wakefield are up to by joining the Sweet Valley High® Fan Club for the one-year membership fee of only $6.25 each for U.S. residents, $8.25 for Canadian residents (U.S. currency). Includes shipping & handling.

Send a check or money order (do not send cash) made payable to "Sweet Valley High® Fan Club" along with this form to:

SWEET VALLEY HIGH® FAN CLUB, BOX 3919-B, SCHAUMBURG, IL 60168-3919

NAME_____
(Please print clearly)

ADDRESS_____

CITY_____ STATE _____ ZIP_____
(Required)

AGE_____ BIRTHDAY_____ /_____ /_____

Offer good while supplies last. Allow 6-8 weeks after check clearance for delivery. Addresses without ZIP codes cannot be honored. Offer good in USA & Canada only. Void where prohibited by law.
©1993 by Francine Pascal   LCI-1383-123

DG-1